I0557573

Smith's MONTHLY

*Every Month Original
Novels, Stories, and Articles*

USA Today Bestselling Writer
Dean Wesley Smith

TABLE OF CONTENTS

Smith's Monthly Issue #16

All Contents copyright © 2015 Dean Wesley Smith
Published by WMG Publishing
Cover and interior design copyright © 2015 WMG Publishing
Cover art copyright © by Mskorpion/Dreamstime.com and Evaners/Dreamstime.com

"Introduction: Marching Forward" copyright © 2015 Dean Wesley Smith

"Living Time" copyright © 2015 Dean Wesley Smith, cover design copyright © 2015 WMG Publishing, cover photo by Cornelius20/Dreamstime.com

"Miss Smallwood's Goodies" copyright © 2015 Dean Wesley Smith, cover design copyright © 2015 WMG Publishing, cover photo by Rudolf Tittelbach/Dreamstime.com

They're Back copyright © 2015 Dean Wesley Smith, cover design copyright © 2015 WMG Publishing, cover art by Polygraphus/Dreamstime.com

"Nostalgia 101" copyright © 2015 Dean Wesley Smith, cover design copyright © 2015 WMG Publishing, cover art by Angela Harburn/Dreamstime.com

"She Arrived Without a Song" copyright © 2015 Dean Wesley Smith, cover design copyright © 2015 WMG Publishing, cover art by Selestron76/Dreamstime.com

"A Vanilla Three-Way with a Cherry" copyright © 2015 Dean Wesley Smith, cover design copyright © 2015 WMG Publishing, cover art by Citalliance/Dreamstime.com

Cold Call: A Cold Poker Gang novel copyright © 2015 Dean Wesley Smith, cover design copyright © 2015 WMG Publishing, cover art by Mskorpion/Dreamstime.com and Evaners/Dreamstime.com

*This book is licensed for your personal enjoyment only. All rights reserved.
This is a work of fiction. All characters and events portrayed in the fiction in this book are fictional, and any resemblance to real people or incidents is purely coincidental.
This book, or parts thereof, may not be reproduced in any form without permission.*

The Writings and Opinions of

Dean Wesley Smith

Introduction
MARCHING FORWARD

IT'S JANUARY and off we go into a brand new year.

Sometimes new years just don't do much for me, other times the promise of the unknown excites me.

I am excited about this coming new year not because of unknowns, but because a lot of good things are happening in WMG Publishing and with my writing.

And honestly, I'm excited that I'm keeping this magazine going into a new year. I see no sign of this magazine ending any time in the near future.

Of course, since it's my magazine, there will be some changes as time goes along, but that's the fun, at least for me. I figure if I can keep myself entertained in these pages, it will entertain you as well.

As I write this introduction, I finished the novel for the next issue. So the writing just keeps on marching forward as well into the future.

The novel in this issue is a Thunder Mountain novel. I have been very challenged writing those complex time travel novels. I hope you enjoy the novel here because it adds brand new dimensions and characters to the Thunder Mountain world.

I also have five short stories in this issue. So if you have read all sixteen issues of this magazine, you will have read 16 novels, two serial novels, a nonfiction golf humor book, and 70 short stories. That's a lot of reading.

And all sixteen issues are still available in any normal bookstore in paper and electronic editions. So never too late to get started.

So here is my hope for this New Year.

—Twelve new issues of this magazine, counting this one, which will include another sixty or so short stories, more serial novels, and articles and poems.

—Six new volumes of the WMG Publishing magazine *Fiction River*.

Thanks for the Support

Dean Wesley Smith

—I hope to keep teaching and putting together new online workshops and lectures to help fiction writers get started with their dreams of writing.

—I hope to help WMG Publishing with a lot of projects, including our new brick-and-mortar store that we bought in October.

—I hope to do a little traveling to teach and for enjoyment. WMG Publishing sponsored a scholarship for a writer attending another workshop in Colorado this last month, and I hope we can do more of that as well.

And so much more.

It's going to be a very busy year.

Thank you for sticking with the ups and downs of the first sixteen issues of this magazine. I hope you have enjoyed the stories and novels and articles here. It has been my pleasure to write them and present them to you.

So I'm marching forward into another year.

I plan on having a lot of fun. I hope you'll stay with me for the ride.

—*Dean Wesley Smith*
January 8th, 2015
Lincoln City, Oregon

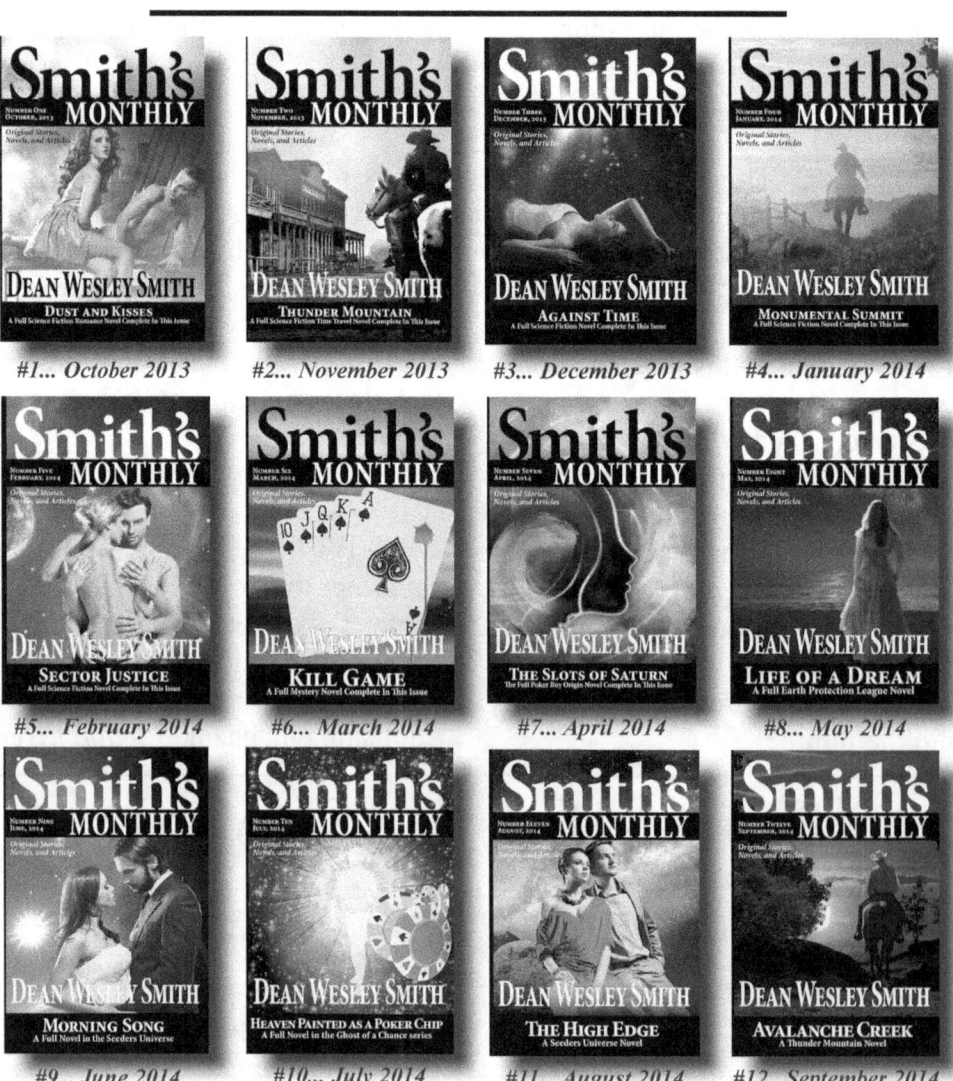

#1... October 2013   #2... November 2013   #3... December 2013   #4... January 2014

#5... February 2014   #6... March 2014   #7... April 2014   #8... May 2014

#9... June 2014   #10... July 2014   #11... August 2014   #12...September 2014

Coming Next Issue in Smith's Monthly
A return to the Thunder Mountain Series
in a brand new novel.
WARM SPRINGS

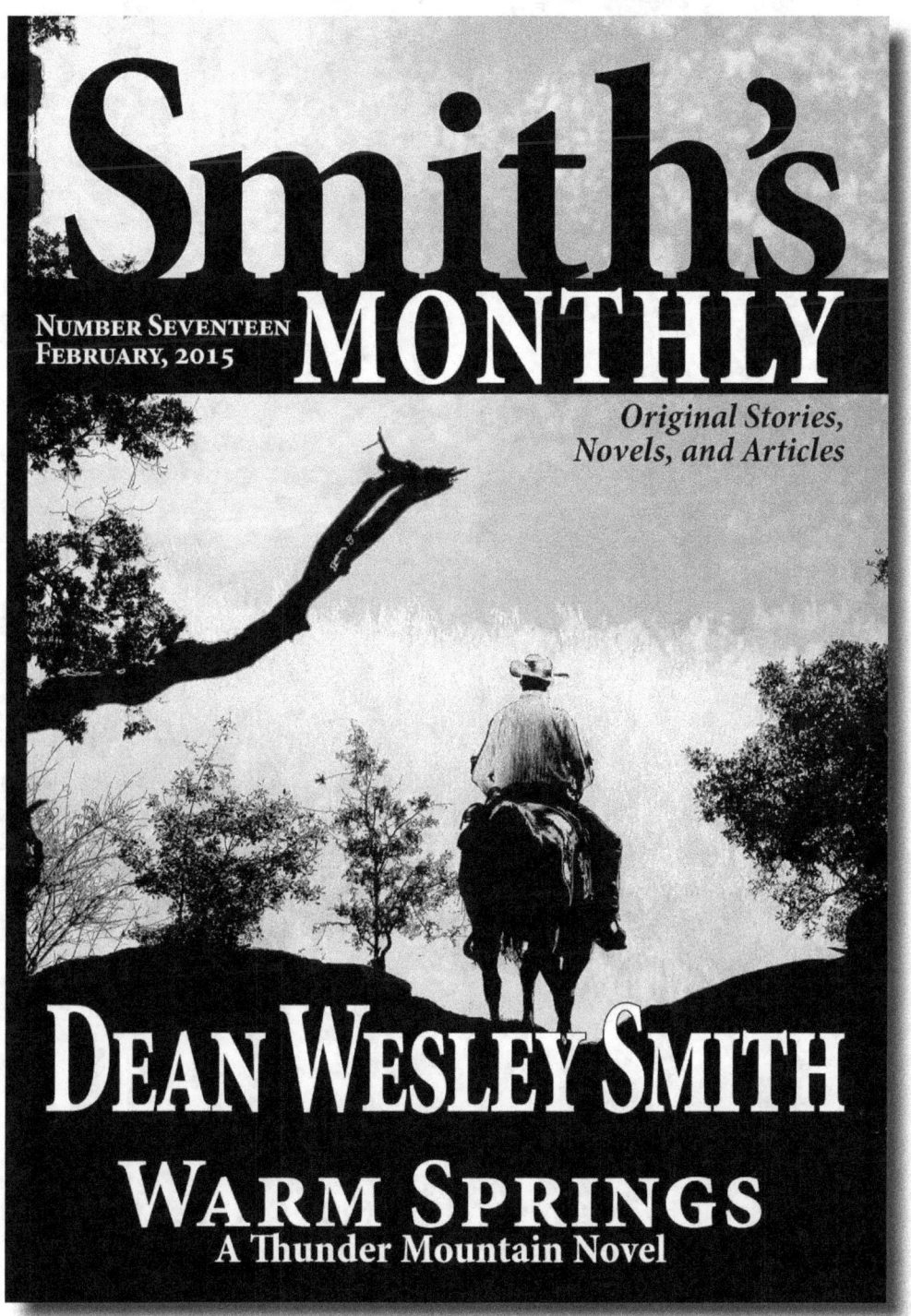

In a casino in Oregon, Poker Boy beats a man fair-and-square at the poker table while a stranger watches, a stranger who knows too much about Poker Boy and his job.

It turns out that much of Poker Boy's future rested on that one hand of cards.

A classic Poker Boy story with true heart.

LIVING TIME
A Poker Boy Story

ONE

I SAT under the gaze of some idiot who had watched too much poker on television as he stared at me like he knew what he was doing. I have no idea what he was looking for, and I had no doubt he didn't know either, but he kept it up, trying to decide if he should toss in his last two hundred bucks and call my bet.

He had on a heavy wool sweater and had taped one side of his glasses with white tape. The longer he stared at me, the more he sweated. He was in the third chair and I was in the sixth. The two men between us had both scooted their chairs back to stay out of the way of the showdown.

Around us the Spirit Winds Casino poker room was doing a good business for ten o'clock on a Thursday night in the middle of January. Five tables were going, including two no-limit tables and from the looks of it there was a waiting list on the board.

The noises from the slots and black-jack tables filtered into the room like a steady background of white noise and two of the televisions in the corners were on, both showing different professional basketball games.

A couple players were sitting at empty tables just watching the games.

I had two more hours before I needed to jump from the Oregon mountains to Las Vegas using my new teleportation power to pick up my girlfriend, Patty Ledgerwood, aka Front Desk Girl, from her job at the MGM Grand Hotel on the Strip. So I was enjoying a friendly game picking up a few hundred here and there along the way.

In two hours it had been a profitable night, a large part because of the guy staring at me. He had started with almost a grand and was down to his last two hundred of the two racks of five-dollar chips he had sat down with.

Outside the Casino the night felt like it would snow at any moment and the wind was biting and cold. In Vegas the temperature would be in the low fifties at midnight when I picked up Patty.

At some point I was going to just move to Vegas, buy or build a place there. But I still liked this casino and the area around it and considered this casino my home casino, even though I didn't spend much time these days in my doublewide trailer a few miles from here.

In fact, I couldn't remember the last night I had slept there. It hadn't been since Patty and I got more serious and I learned how to teleport. And that had been a good six months.

Down the table the guy just kept watching me, sweating, trying to decide what to do. I had a pair of aces down and there was an ace and two deuces on the board with a king. I doubted he had a pair of deuces in his hand, otherwise he would have called me at once and laughed while flipping his cards over.

More than likely he had the 4th ace and a bad kicker. He might have a king and was wondering if I had an ace. Either way I had him beat and beat badly.

I smiled at him, tipping back my black Fedora-like hat.

"Anything I can tell you?" I asked him, smiling.

The dealer frowned, but said nothing.

The guy just shook his head, checked his cards again, then went back to staring at me.

The more he sweated and stared, the more I stared to sense the guy had a problem larger than this hand. He was playing with money he couldn't afford to lose. I had figured that much out earlier, and now I was about to take his last few hundred. The sweat on his forehead was for a lot more than just a hand and a couple hundred dollars. To this guy, he thought he was betting his entire life.

And at a poker table, that never worked out well. Poker could be a very cruel game, especially when you shouldn't be playing.

He stared and stared, the sweat beading on his forehead and his eyes slits behind his broken glasses. More than likely he had read some stupid book on poker tells and was trying to watch me for one. So I decided to give him a tell from the first chapter.

I leaned forward, pretending to want to flip my cards over and show him. The book said that if a player acted strong, they had a weak hand. I honestly didn't care if he called me or not. I just wanted the stupid hand over.

He smiled. "You don't have it," he said. "You're bluffing."

He pushed in his last two hundred bucks and then waited for me to flip over my cards. If he had flipped his cards over I might have mucked and just given him the hand and the money, but he didn't.

I flipped over my two aces and his face went pale.

"Might want to read that book again," I said as the dealer shoved the pile of chips my way.

The guy beside the loser on the end of the table just shook his head. "You should know better than to mess with Poker Boy."

I glanced at the guy again, pretending I wasn't upset that he knew my superhero name. But I was.

The dealer glanced at me, then went back to gathering the cards to shuffle.

I didn't like it that someone had used my superhero name here, in my home casino. I didn't like it at all.

I had a read on the guy from his play over the last two hours. Strong player, cautious, no real tells. He was someone to be very careful with. More than likely he was a pro. Of the chips that had come across the table in the last two hours, I had a large number of them and he had the rest.

He wore a tan Izod golf shirt and had put his ski parka on a hook beside the door. He had brown short hair and brown eyes and a slightly hooked nose. He looked to be about thirty, but I could be off in either direction by a decade.

He looked to be about my height at six foot. But he looked stronger, with wider, football-player-like shoulders and neck.

He was nothing exceptional and except for his play, he had stayed under my radar for the two hours he had been at the table. I had just not paid him much attention.

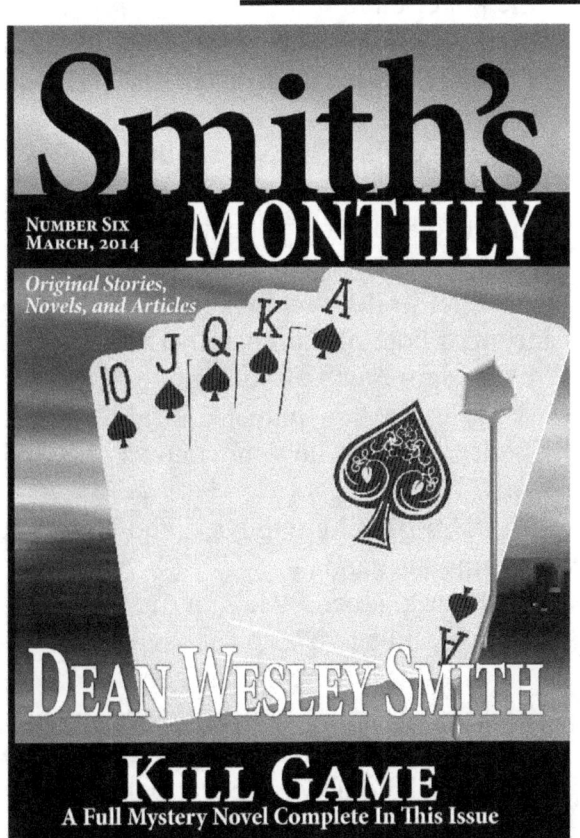

Don't Miss an Issue!

Subscribe

Electronic Subscription:
6 Issues... $29.99
12 Issues... $49.99

Paper Subscription:
6 Issues... $59.99
12 Issues... $99.99

For Full Subscription Information Go To:

www.SmithsMonthly.com

Impressive.

"Have we met?" I asked as I stacked the chips, knowing for a fact that we had never met before. I did not forget a face. I had trouble with names, but never a face. That was part of my superpowers. And as a poker player, I know I would have re-membered him from his play.

"Nope," the guy said, smiling. "Stan sent me."

My stomach flipped, but I kept stack-ing my chips trying to get some sort of read on the situation.

The loser beside him finally decided he was done and shoved his chair back, clearly angry at his loss.

"I hope you two are proud of yourselves," he said looking at me, then at the guy I had been talking to. "I know collusion when I see it."

The guy I had been talking to who claimed Stan had sent him reached over casually and just touched the arm of the guy. "We're just having a friendly game here," he said. "Nothing out of the ordinary, I can promise you."

The guy sort of stood there for a mo-ment, then shook his head and laughed. "Yeah, I know that. Just sort of mad at my own stupid play."

Wow! The guy had some powers! I was stunned.

"Actually," the guy said to the angry man, "you are a pretty damn fine player. You just ran into the best tonight."

The guy nodded. "Thanks, appreciate that." He looked at me, smiled and said, "Nice playing with you."

Then the guy walked off as I stared at the guy who knew my name. I felt I should follow the guy out to see what he planned to do after his loss, but at that moment I was more concerned with the guy across from me who knew my name.

"You said Stan sent you?" I asked. "Which Stan?"

"Your boss of course," the guy said, smiling.

TWO

I INSTANTLY took the two of us out of time, freezing everyone else in the room. All the sounds of the casino van-ished and everyone stayed in place, stuck between two moments in time.

Except the two of us.

"Wow, nifty trick," the guy said, his eyes large as he looked around. "I hope I can learn how to do that someday."

"Stan!" I shouted at the ceiling as I stood and moved a few steps away from the poker table.

A moment later Stan, the God of Poker, appeared in front of me. He was wearing his normal tan slacks, tan shirt and sweater and he was smiling.

"Good," he said to me. "I see you've met The Kid. How'd he do?"

"What do you mean by that?"

Stan smiled and looked at the chips in front of both of our chairs. "Doesn't look like he got much of your money."

"He's a fine player," I said. "I just want to know how he knows me and you?"

"I'm right here, guys," The Kid said, waving his hand.

Stan laughed. "He's the new recruit. So how did he do?"

"Besides blurting out my name in front of an entire table, and mentioning your name, and being way too old to be called kid, he played decent poker."

Stan looked at The Kid and shook his head. "You never say another superhero's name out loud in front of regular people."

"Sorry," The Kid said, actually looking worried and sheepish. "I didn't know."

Stan laughed and waved it off. "You'll learn."

I couldn't begin to count the times Stan had used those same words with me in my first few years as a superhero. And now that I was actually looking at The Kid, he did look a lot younger than my first take on his age. At most he was twenty-five. It was a nifty trick being able to shift his age appearance like that. I would have to learn it.

"New recruit?" I asked Stan. "Working for you?"

"Yup," Stan said, smiling. "Laverne approved it and everything. She said you and your team are doing more work for all of the gods and I needed the help with just poker."

"I told you that last week," I said, smiling at him.

I walked over to The Kid and stuck out my hand as he stood from the table. "Nice meeting you, Kid."

"The honor is all mine, Poker Boy," The Kid said, smiling and shaking my hand like I was a rock star. "You are the smoothest player I have ever had the honor to sit with."

"You ain't half bad yourself," I said. "And nice job staying hidden as long as you did."

"Thanks," he said, beaming.

I remembered in my early years how important it was to have someone tell me I did something right. Hell, after ten years now, it was still important. I doubt it would ever get old.

USA Today *bestselling writer Dean Wesley Smith returns with a second novel to the world of* Dust and Kisses *from the first issue of* Smith's Monthly.

Together, Callie and Fisher work to discover the secrets of a galaxy that have been hidden in plain sight, even from the powerful humans who had rescued millions.

And in the process, they just might change everything.

Now Available
from all your favorite booksellers in trade paper and electronic editions.

Then I got serious as I turned back to Stan. "I can handle it from here," I said. "We have some work to do."

"Give him time," Stan said to me. "Don't push too hard."

"I promise," I said.

Stan vanished and I turned back to The Kid. "Come with me. We have a problem to clean up."

The kid looked puzzled, but followed me through the frozen people and the silence of the casino.

"This is just creepy," he said, staring at a woman chewing on a large hotdog, her mouth open and full of half-eaten bun.

About halfway across the casino I found who I was looking for. The guy who had been at the table on that last hand. I had taken the last of his money.

"Did you sense any problem with this guy?" I asked The Kid.

"He was desperate, playing with important money. That's why I tried to calm him some."

"And you did fine with that, but my sense is that what you did won't be enough. I may be wrong, but if I'm not, I want to make sure nothing goes too wrong."

The Kid looked puzzled, but only nodded.

"Now, let's get back to the table so I can put us in real time again. Follow my lead."

THREE

WHEN WE were both seated, I put us back into the natural flow of time. The sounds of the casino smashed into us.

"Let's go talk," I said to The Kid and pushed my chair back.

"Glad to," he said. Then to the dealer he said, "We'll be right back."

The dealer nodded and began dealing to the other six at the table.

The Kid stayed with me as we left the poker room.

"Dead camera area here," I said and jumped us to a dead camera area in the parking lot.

The Kid looked stunned. "Wow, do I have a lot to learn."

"Give it time," I said, heading toward the front door of the casino.

A moment later the guy who had tried to get a read on me came out of the front door and turned to the left toward one of the parking lots. When he got there, he climbed into an old Ford that looked like it had seen its better days.

Then he just sat behind the wheel as if he had no place to go.

More than likely, if my sense of him was right, he didn't.

The Kid and I stood off to one side near a truck so we could watch him and not be seen. I had on my black leather coat and hat that was my superhero uniform, but I could still feel the cold wind. The Kid was in a short-sleeved golf shirt and he was shaking already.

"You might want to learn to always wear a jacket of some sort in a poker room," I said. "Both for sitting under air-conditioning and for this job."

"I'll remember that," he said, his teeth almost chattering.

"Where you from?" I asked.

"Southern California," he said.

"You want to go back in for your coat?"

He shook his head. "I'll make it."

At that moment the guy in the car moved. But he didn't go to turn on his car. Instead, he reached over to his glove box and opened it and pulled out what looked to be a pistol of some type.

"Shit, he's going to off himself," The Kid said, starting to run at the car.

I jumped us out of time again, then called for The Kid to hold on. He stopped and waited for me.

"I really need to learn how to do that," he said.

Then he followed me over to the car as I opened the car door, took the gun from the guy's hand, unloaded the clip, made sure there was no round anywhere in the gun, then put the gun back in the guy's hand, closed the door and indicated that The Kid should follow me away from the car.

"You were sure right about the guy," he said. "How did you know?"

"Just reading people," I said.

We got back to where we had been and I let us go back into the flow of time. The wind again hit us hard and The Kid shivered.

"Follow my lead completely," I said and he nodded as we started back toward the guy's car.

He didn't see us coming. He just kept staring at the gun in his hands until I knocked on the window and startled him.

He tried to hide the gun by dropping it on the floor before he opened the car door and stepped out into the cold.

"Yeah," he said. "So you two really are together."

"Not really," I said. "In fact, we just met tonight at the table, but we were both worried about you."

"You are the only people on the planet who are," he said, the sarcasm clear in his voice. "Thanks."

He was in even worse shape than I thought.

I turned on what I call my "empathy-power" and directed it at the guy. And also the power I call "tell-me-the-truth." With both of those powers directed at the poor guy, he had no choice but to tell me what was going on like I was a trusted counselor he had poured his heart out to for years.

"So how bad is it?" I asked. "What's happening?"

"No job, my wife left me six months ago, I'm homeless, and you took the last of my money. I don't even have gas money to get off this stupid mountain and back to Portland. That's how bad."

"That's bad," I said, nodding.

Beside me The Kid nodded, but said nothing.

"So what did you do for a living?" I asked.

He laughed. "What every other unemployed person around this area did. I worked construction. Actually, I had my own construction business, had a dozen guys working for me, building some of the best custom homes in Oregon. Bobby C. Davis Construction."

He said the name of his business with pride and I suddenly had a great idea to help this guy not put the barrel of that gun in his mouth.

I laughed. "Great meeting you," I said and extended my hand. "I'm Gary Barnes."

Gary Barnes was one of my fake names I used in the real world when I had to. Actually, everyone around this casino called me Gary and my doublewide trailer a couple miles away was under that name as well.

The kid stepped forward to shake the guy's hand. "I'm Roger Stevens," he said.

I had a hunch that was a made-up name by The Kid as well.

"Bob Davis," the guy said, now even more puzzled.

I kept the empathy power turned on high and focused at him and then also turned on my "trust-me" power. This poor guy was putty in my hands, especially in his depressed condition. Luckily, I only used my powers for good.

"I actually looked for your business a few months back," I said, lying through my teeth. I was a poker player. Lying was part of our job description. "I've been wanting to build a custom home on some property I have near here, a big, beautiful custom home, and your firm was recommended to me a number of times."

"Really?" he asked, smiling. Then his mood turned again. "See how quality work turns out?" He pointed at the old car he was driving. "I sold my rig and most of my tools to get living money and money to pay my child support. I hoped to win enough tonight to make next month's payment and get a little apartment. That went well as you know."

"How old are your children?" The Kid asked, expertly moving the subject from the guy's loss to something better.

The guy seemed to melt at the mention of them. "Six and eight," he said.

"I think they would rather have their father than money," I said.

He shrugged, but I could tell he wasn't so sure.

FOUR

"TELL YOU WHAT, BOB," I said. "How about you go to work for me and my girlfriend and build us the house of our dreams?" I sure hoped Patty had some

idea of what would make a good custom home. I didn't.

He looked at me and then smiled, but shook his head. "I don't have the tools or even a truck or a place to stay."

"None of that's a problem," I said, laughing. "I need someone with your skill. I've got a doublewide close to here that I'm not using that you can live in for free, and I'll fund you for a new truck and tools. Besides that, I'll put you on a regular salary for as long as it takes to build the house. And from what Patty and I want, that might take some time. All custom."

We all three stood there in the cold wind as he stared at me, again trying to get a read on me.

Luckily, this time it didn't take as long as at the poker table.

"Are you for real?" he asked. "You can't really be scamming me. I've got nothing more anyone could take."

"I'm not kidding," I said. "I was hoping to hire someone with your skill to build me a house here and from the looks of your situation, I can get you cheaper than you used to charge. A good deal for me."

With that he laughed. "Yeah, a bunch cheaper, to be honest."

"Do we have a deal?" I asked, extending my hand. "You come to work for me and build me the best damn place you can. And maybe by the time you're done, the economy will have turned a little and you can ramp your business back up. Or come down to Vegas and help me build a house there after you're done here."

He hesitated for only a moment, looking me right in the eyes, and then he nodded and shook my hand, smiling. "We have a deal. Thanks. You need to know you just saved my life."

"Actually," I said, waving off his thank you. "You just saved me from moving away from a place I love. But we have to make one more agreement."

"What's that?" he asked, looking suddenly worried.

"You won't come in here while you work for me to do anything but have dinner. You're a fine poker player, but you need to play for the right reasons."

"Deal," he said, smiling. "And after we get the house done, maybe you can give me some lessons."

"That I can do," I said, smiling.

I handed him a few hundred dollars and pointed at the gas station and grocery across the highway. "This is an advance. I'm going to go cash out my chips. You need to get some gas and some food to stock a fridge for later and breakfast. There's not a damn thing in that doublewide. Meet me back here in twenty minutes."

"Got it, boss," he said, smiling, the look of desperation now completely gone from his eyes, replaced with a glimmer of hope.

Halfway back across the cold parking lot, The Kid finally broke his silence. "That felt great helping him like that. Is that what it's like being a superhero?"

"Sometimes, yeah, it is. On the good nights."

We walked a little ways in silence again before he asked the next question.

"You really wanted to build a house up here?"

I laughed. "I hadn't actually thought of it until tonight. But I own some nice land on hills around here as well as my doublewide. And Patty, my girlfriend, won't stay up here with me because my place is so shabby. So I might as well build a house with her help so she'll come up here at times."

"You like it here that much?" The Kid asked as we got close to the front doors.

"I do," I said.

"So you saved a man's life and helped yourself at the same time. You are good. Both at poker and at life."

"Is there much difference?" I asked, repeating a phrase that Stan once said to me when I was starting out.

"Not when you play them both the way you do," The Kid said, holding the front door of the Casino open for me.

And that was one of the nicest things anyone had said to me in a long time. I was going to like this kid.

~

Some Classic Dean Wesley Smith Stories
Available at your favorite booksellers.

Dean Wesley Smith

USA Today Bestselling Writer

A
PILGRIM HUGH
INCIDENT

MISS SMALLWOOD'S
GOODIES

Sent to investigate the sudden appearance of the statue of a naked woman in a park, Pilgrim Hugh must first decide if placing a statue without permission constitutes a crime?

And why the statue of the naked woman lost all her personal parts? Are those missing personal parts the answer to the origin of the statue?

Another strange Pilgrim Hugh Incident.

MISS SMALLWOOD'S GOODIES
A Pilgrim Hugh Incident

ONE

PILGRIM HUGH stared at the lifelike statue of the naked and blue woman.

Actually, she wasn't completely naked. She wore a large cowboy hat and carried a large revolver in her right hand pointed upward. Her finger was on the trigger like she was about to blow a hole in the rim of her hat.

The last days of summer were just starting to fade, but the temperature for the Portland, Oregon, area still seemed too high at eighty-five. The statue stood in a park in a suburban town of Portland called Hillsboro. The Chief of Police of Hillsboro had called Pilgrim to figure out where the statue had come from. The statue seemed to have just appeared late last night and a couple mothers of small children had complained this morning.

Hillsboro, it seemed, wasn't used to getting statues donated to their parks in the middle of the night.

Over the last few years as a freelance private detective and lawyer, Pilgrim had gotten some strange calls, and this was another of the strange ones, of that there was no doubt.

After he'd gotten out of law school, he had tried to work in corporate law. He had managed two years, the exact same amount of time his first marriage lasted. Basically he had become bored with both.

Then his grandmother on his long-dead mother's side, a woman he barely knew, died and left him more money than even he could imagine or try to spend.

Two months after being divorced and out of work he had become free to do what he wanted.

His choice, as any young person might do, was a year of drinking and traveling around the world. Somewhere in the alcoholic haze, there was another even shorter marriage.

Eventually he went back to school to become a private detective, figuring that wouldn't be as boring as the law practice.

Most of the training was not like the books about private detectives he loved to read. In fact most of what he had done was learn how to track someone by computer and look up financial records.

Finally, out of desperation to do something interesting, he set up his own combination law and private detective firm, hired a couple of talented associate lawyers to handle the really boring cases, and offered his services for free to the different city police departments around the Portland metropolitan area.

Hugh and Associates now occupied three floors in a downtown Portland high-rise. He had started out rich from his grandmother and managed to get even richer by hiring the right people and taking the right cases over the last few years.

Carrie, Pilgrim's assistant, limo driver, and best friend, stood beside him, staring at the blue statue. Today Carrie had on a green University of Oregon sweatshirt (that didn't hide her figure much at all) and a pair of white shorts that also hid little. Even in her late thirties, she could still have been modeling.

Pilgrim was over six feet tall and Carrie usually seemed to tower over him because of tall heels. But today they were the same height since she had on a rare pair of tennis shoes that matched her outfit perfectly.

Carrie was about to finish her last year of law school at the University of Oregon and join the legal side of Pilgrim's firm. But until that day, she paid for her apartment and food and school by being his assistant and driver when she wasn't in class.

He was going to miss her when her last year of law school started back up later in the month. They were such a good team.

The statue was anchored to what looked like a concrete slab and on the face of the slab was a name. "Miss Smallwood."

"Very lifelike," Carrie said, moving around the statue.

The blue statue did look very, very lifelike. No question there. Except the skin was perfectly smooth, the naked breasts had no nipples and were perfectly smooth, and the crotch of the statue looked like it came from a doll, also perfectly smooth with no attempt to make it lifelike in any way.

The eyes were open, yet showed no detail.

The entire thing felt creepy. Even in the bright sunlight and hot day.

TWO

THE PARK that now held the Miss Smallwood statue was only one block wide and a block long, surrounded by a sidewalk. A few other sidewalks wound into the trees and to a new playground in the far corner. A very nice neighborhood park, very well maintained.

The statue had been placed near the sidewalk facing an apartment complex across the street. In fact, it seemed to really be staring at that apartment building.

Pilgrim looked over at it, following the direction of the statue's look. The apartment looked to be a renovated old hotel of some sort. Stone and brick exterior, large windows. A nice place from the looks of it.

Pilgrim moved over and stared at the large revolver in the statue's hand. It looked real and from what he could tell the artist had depicted it with one shell missing.

"Know anything about guns?" Pilgrim asked Carrie.

"It's a revolver," Carrie said. "That's about it."

Pilgrim laughed. "I knew that much."

"Frank from the estate planning part of your office is a gun nut," Carrie said. "You want me to send him a picture?"

"Might as well," Pilgrim said. He doubted it would make any difference but it never hurt to get the details together.

Carrie started back toward the limo that served as an office for them. Pilgrim had every possible modern device he could think of in that car, from high-speed computer connections to sophisticated camera and listening equipment.

He moved closer and tapped the hard surface of the statue. It felt like a plastic resin of some sort.

He moved around the statue, studying every tiny detail. Clearly the statue had been made by a mold. And then polished and finished with a clear, thick blue resin compound. The resin looked to be almost a quarter inch thick in some places.

Fantastic work. Not a mark or seam anywhere.

The statue was clearly made from the mold of a real woman. Her legs were slightly too long for her final height, her hips just a touch too wide, and the right breast was slightly larger than the other.

A perfect statue, no marks at all, yet not a perfect woman as the subject.

Pilgrim stepped back and realized he was shivering slightly even with the heat of the day.

This statue just flat gave him the creeps.

He walked in a large circle around the statue, just trying to let his mind take in the details. It had been placed near the entrance to the park, between where a sidewalk split. But it hadn't been placed looking directly at the walkway, but instead at a slight angle staring off at the nearby apartment across the street.

With as perfect as this statue was done, why mess up the placement? Pilgrim would bet it wasn't messed up. It was intentional.

Carrie came back with the camera, snapped a couple of close-ups of the revolver in the statue's hand and then sent the images from the camera back to the office.

Then she put the camera down and picked up what looked like an iPad and aimed it at the statue.

"Shit!" she said, staring at the device in her hands.

"What?" Pilgrim asked, moving over toward her.

She had turned her back on the statue and was clearly trying to catch her breath.

"You all right?" he asked.

She shook her head yes, then showed him the image on the device.

"I wanted to see what the inside of the statue looked like," she said.

All Pilgrim could do was stare at the image on the device. No wonder the statue wasn't perfect. It was an actual woman inside that resin.

He could see every detail of her skeleton. Her insides had been cleaned out like they did with embalming. Metal bars ran up both legs. Another was up her spine and through her neck to hold her head.

Pilgrim turned to look at the woman frozen like a statue. "Whoever did this cut off the woman's nipples and smoothed over any sign."

"And covered or removed her crotch as well," Carrie said. "And covered or removed her eyes."

"Took and kept all the goodies," Carrie said.

"Better call Chief Benson," Pilgrim said, "tell him he has a crime scene here. The statue isn't a statue, it's a body."

"He's going to love this," Carrie said. "To find the killer he has to look for a woman's nipples and crotch."

"Might not want to tell him that on the phone," Pilgrim said.

"Not a chance," Carrie said, heading for the limo again, picking up the camera along the way.

THREE

PILGRIM DID another slow walk about the woman's body, looking at it with a new perspective. He was convinced that the placement in this park, in that exact position had something to do with all this.

He needed to find out what she was looking at with those blank eyes.

He headed back for the coolness of the limo and crawled into the back just as Carrie hung up. "Detectives and crime scene crew on the way. Benson said he would be here in fifteen minutes and we're not to move."

"Yeah, I bet," Pilgrim said.

"So," Carrie said, "any idea on The Case of Miss Smallwood's Goodies?"

Carrie loved to give each of the investigations they did a strange case name that almost always stuck.

"Some," Pilgrim said. "Search the area databases for a woman of that height and size and age being reported missing in the last month. Might want to go all the way down to San Francisco and up to Seattle as well in the search."

"Got it," Carrie said.

She was sitting with her back to the front compartment and a large computer complex of keyboards and screens opened out of the seat beside her, sliding out to almost surround where she was sitting with a keyboard on her lap and a large screen in front of her.

Pilgrim was on the seat near the wet bar. He turned and punched a hidden button on the bar, letting it turn into another computer center with a large screen and two small screens where the drinks had been.

He loved this limo. He felt like a superhero at times. The car was the most sophisticated computer center on wheels that he knew of. He loved it and never once questioned the costs to build it and keep it completely outfitted with any new device that would help him with a case.

In this car he could almost see through walls, hear something whispered two hundred yards away, and tap into any phone line he wanted to. This was a dream car for any private detective.

He immediately typed in the address of the apartment complex the woman statue was looking at.

Then on one screen he pulled up a floor plan of the building and on the other a list of tenants.

The landlord, a man by the name of Steven Frome, lived in a large apartment on the main floor with his wife, Sue. It was the only apartment on the first floor; the rest of the space was filled with a large lobby and entrance area. He had been right, the building had been an old hotel at one time in the past called The Wellington Inn. It had been converted to apartments in 1962 and Frome had bought it in 2001.

There was nothing in the full basement that showed on the floor plan and four apartments per floor from the second floor through the fifth, all fairly large.

Pilgrim couldn't see anything at all odd about any of the tenants or the building or the landlord.

"No missing person meets her look, size, or shape," Carrie said, "anywhere in the Pacific Northwest in the last six months."

"Yeah, that would have been too easy," Pilgrim said, shaking his head.

"So why would someone do this to a person and put them in this park?"

Carrie asked as outside the first police car arrived on the scene.

"Figure that out and I bet we find Miss Smallwood's goodies," Pilgrim said. "I'll go talk to the police. Bring up pictures and background checks of anyone in that building there. I'll bet anything there is a reason she's looking in that direction."

Carrie nodded and went to work as Pilgrim crawled back out in to the heat.

"Where's the body?" the dark, heavyset policeman asked. His name on his uniform was Wells.

Pilgrim pointed at the shiny, blue statue that seemed to be glistening in the sunlight as if she was sweating, even with the big cowboy hat and revolver.

"You're kidding?" Officer Wells asked. "That statue?"

"I wish I was," Pilgrim said.

Pilgrim went back to staring at the statue for a moment as Officer Wells started to tape off the area. More than likely the hat and gun the woman had were clues as well, but damn if Pilgrim could even figure out how to start on them.

At that moment Chief of Police Benson pulled up and got out into the heat.

"You're telling me that's a body?" he asked, as Pilgrim met him halfway across the lawn toward the statue.

"Sealed in resin and disguised, yes," Pilgrim said.

"You mean like that traveling science exhibit where bodies were frozen in movement in some sort of resin. The one that showed all the body's muscles and other parts most of us didn't want to see or even know about?"

"Might be like that," Pilgrim said, shaking his head. "I didn't know you were into science, Chief?"

"The kid loves the Omsi Center. That exhibit just grossed me out and I've seen a lot of bodies in my day." Chief Benson stopped a few feet from the statue. "What happened to her nipples and crotch?"

"The killer must have wanted to keep them. Or thought them too private to show," Pilgrim said.

Suddenly he realized what he had just said. The missing parts were the answer after all.

FOUR

"HANG ON, CHIEF. I'm not so sure this is a crime after all. At least not a murder."

Pilgrim turned and headed back for the limo with Chief Benson right behind him.

Inside the cool interior, the Chief sighed as he closed the door. "I sure wish the city would spring for one of these for me."

"More than the city budget for a year," Carrie said, not looking up from the computer screen in front of her.

"Carrie," Pilgrim said, "can you do a search of death notices in the last year. Pictures of woman the age of the statue out there."

"Sure," Carrie said, frowning.

While she was doing that, Pilgrim looked up the occupations of all the tenants in the building, including the landlord.

He found exactly as he figured he would find. Steven Frome, the owner of the building, owned three of the area funeral homes.

"Look for a death notice for Sue Frome," Pilgrim said to Carrie.

"Already found her," Carrie said, swinging around he computer screen showing a picture of Sue Frome. "Maiden name Smallwood."

There was no doubt it was the woman in the statue.

"She died three months ago of terminal brain cancer," Carrie said. "She went very quickly. In fact, this park is named after her since her husband donated a ton of money in her memory to upgrade it and put in new kid's swings and such."

"He made her into a statue and stuck her here?" Benson asked. "Creepy."

"Death makes people do strange things at times," Pilgrim said.

"She liked to spend time in the park her last weeks," Carrie said. "And she was a top shot and loved to ride horses. All in the obituary."

"That explains the gun and the hat," Pilgrim said, nodding.

'Oh, shit, now what am I supposed to do?" Benson asked. "I'm fairly certain there's a rule against this somewhere."

"I'd go talk to Steven Frome, get him to remove her to a more appropriate place and then put a real statue in her place."

"Yeah, makes sense," Benson said. "Better than the press getting wind of this. Can you imagine the news?"

"Ask him what he did with her goodies," Carrie said as the Chief started to climb out.

"Her what?"

Pilgrim shook his head. "Never mind. Just Carrie's name for this case is all."

"You two are weird," Benson said, smiling. "But thanks."

After Benson got out and the computers were back into their hiding places, Carrie said, "Don't you want to know what happened to the woman's goodies?"

"Not even in the slightest," Pilgrim said, shaking his head. "Curiosity about another man's wife's private parts can only lead to problems."

"And you know this how?" Carrie asked, smiling.

Pilgrim dug out a Diet Coke for himself and handed Carrie a regular Coke. "How about we just let your imagination and memory work on that one while you drive us back to the office."

"You are no fun at all, boss," Carrie said, smiling as she took the offered can and started to climb out of the limo to move up to the front seat.

"That's not what she said," Pilgrim said, smiling.

All Carrie did was groan and then slam the door.

Don't Miss an Issue!
Subscribe

Electronic Subscription:
6 Issues... $29.99
12 Issues... $49.99

Paper Subscription:
6 Issues... $59.99
12 Issues... $99.99

For Full Subscription Information Go To:

www.SmithsMonthly.com

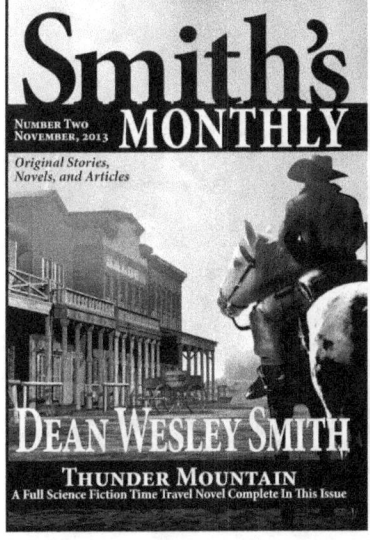

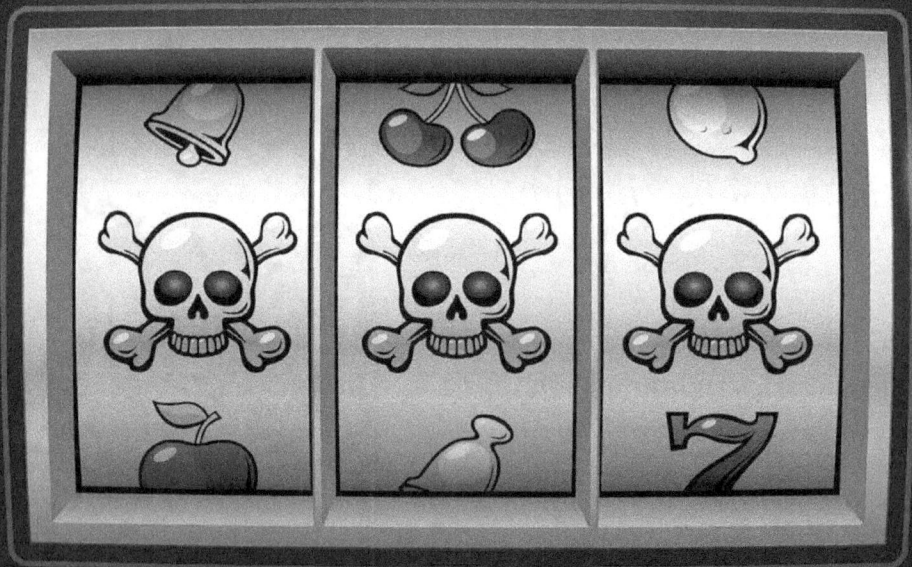

USA Today Bestselling Writer

DEAN WESLEY SMITH

THEY'RE BACK

A Poker Boy Short Novel

In the third of four parts, Poker Boy and his team must confront the worst enemy they ever faced. The dreaded Slots of Saturn once again.

But the Slots of Saturn died years before. How could they be back?

The sequel to the novel The Slots of Saturn, *this short novel appeared first in* Fiction River.

THEY'RE BACK
A Poker Boy Short Novel

Part 3 of 4

CHAPTER ELEVEN
A Second Time Through a Nightmare

WE TOLD MADGE what we were planning and she cleaned off the table and brought us all pads of paper and pens and some fresh glasses of water.

While she was doing that, Sherri and Screamer jumped to her mother to tell her the plan and I called to Stan to come back and I explained the plan to him.

Lady Luck and Stan both thought it was a good idea.

While we were getting set up, Stan got in the list from the Bookkeeper of the names and location his computers told him were the ones from the future we stranded in the past.

I wouldn't let Stan show it to us, since I didn't want what we were about to try to be contaminated in any way.

Stan thought that very smart and agreed. He jumped away to continue to get help from the police on the overall list of names.

So as we all slipped into the booth, we put Screamer in the middle in the back. Sherri was on one side of him and Ben beside her.

Patty was on the other side of Screamer and I was beside her.

Patty and I and Screamer had had our minds together a lot over the years, but this was the first time we had tried it with both Sherri and Ben also in the mix.

"Stay focused on the memory," I said and everyone agreed.

"We start from the first one and go through?" Screamer asked.

"From the first one," I said and he nodded.

Why he had asked about the first one was because the first person out of the machine had been Geneva, a reporter from the *Las Vegas Sun* who we had sent in so that we could communicate with someone inside. She and her boyfriend, a cop friend of mine named Johnny, had developed a very tight mental connection that we used.

I wanted to make sure we didn't get confused in the order and miss anyone.

"Ready for a ride back to hell?" Screamer asked.

Patty and I both nodded.

Sherri took Ben's hand on top of the table and touched Screamer's leg with the other.

Patty touched my leg and then took Screamer's hand on top of the table.

Instantly there were four other people in my head.

I tried to only focus on my memory of that hot day in that graveyard of slot machines.

Patty and Screamer did the same and Sherri sent some waves of calming energy as we were again back in front of those monster machines ten years before.

Ben just felt like a shadow in the distance, watching.

The intense terror I felt overwhelmed me and I could feel Patty's and Screamer's fear as well.

We were standing right in front of the pulsating machines. I was touching Screamer and Patty was holding my hand.

I got the distinct smell of raspberry shampoo, but pushed that thought away and focused on what was about to happen.

Patty had slowed down time and then, slowly, in the chair in front of the right-side slot machine, a woman's body started to materialize seated in the wooden chair.

Screamer reached out when she was complete and shoved her hard out of the way.

I focused on her mind, what was in it, and caught a lot about her and her new relationship with Johnny. More than I thought I could get, actually.

The next person, a woman, started to materialize and I remember thinking how close that was and how fast that was happening, even with Patty slowing time.

Scary fast, Patty thought at me. *I had my eyes closed and hadn't realized it was that close. No wonder you and Screamer have nightmares of people materializing together.*

More than you want to know, Screamer thought at her.

As the woman finished materializing, Screamer pushed her hard out of the way and onto the mat beside the chair. She landed in slow motion on top of Geneva.

The woman's mind seemed open to me. I scanned as much as I could in the fraction of a second Screamer was in contact with her. I could see in her memory that when she was taken by the slots, there was a 2004 Mercedes spinning slowly on some progressive slot machine display to her right. And she was thinking she would really love to win that new car.

Casinos didn't give away old cars, so she was from that time, not today.

The next one out was Ben, the man Patty and I had seen taken from Binion's.

We knew he was fine as well.

Back then we had taken two minutes rests between every group of three, but we didn't need to do that in memory, so we jumped over the two minutes and went through the next three people out of the machine, then did that again with three more.

Then both Patty and Sherri broke their connection with Screamer as we planned.

"Wow, you three were terrified," Sherri said. "I'm impressed you managed to save all those people under that kind of stress and fear. And working with untested superpowers as well. Amazing."

"Thanks for keeping us calm this time through," Screamer said and leaned over and kissed her. "That was a lot better than the first time we had to live that."

I had to agree with him. Sherri was managing to keep the fear in all of us that we felt back then pushed back.

I turned to Ben. "Did you get it all?"

"Every detail," he said. "We start from the first person."

We all grabbed our papers and pens and Ben gave us the first person's full name and when she was born and how she had gotten taken.

As the woman finished materializing, Screamer pushed her hard out of the way and onto the mat beside the chair.

We all agreed on the first one, that what he said matched what we saw as well.

He went on to the second woman, then on to Ben, detailing all three out.

Then he went to the next three, and again all three were taken in 2004. That much was clear, without a doubt.

On each person who it was clear was from 2004, I drew a line through their name on my pad.

It wasn't until we got to number eight out of the machine that we found our first person from this present time.

There was no doubt at all with him.

His name was Willie (William) Jamison. He had been taken as the last one from this time period. He had been twenty-one when taken.

"Oh, no," Patty said as Ben described him.

"What? I asked.

"Remember his face," Patty said. "Do you recognize it?"

"Oh, bloody hell," Screamer said, shaking his head.

I could picture the guy's face and it did look familiar, but darned if I could remember from where.

"He took on the name Ben Williams," Patty said, "back in 2004."

And then it flooded over me. Ben Williams had killed a middle-aged couple in a very brutal and angry fashion in what was called a home invasion. He was found covered in the couple's blood holding their twelve-year-old son. He was sentenced to life in prison and the press said he never showed remorse.

"He was an abused child," Ben said softly. "When he found himself stuck in the past, he had to save his younger self from his own parents."

"And that's why we have alternate realities," Lady Luck said, appearing in front of the booth. "Kronos didn't notice that one forming because it made so little impact, since his parents did nothing and in the main timeline will die not many years from now anyway."

"And the young Willie?" I asked, afraid of the answer.

"He killed himself in foster care at the age of sixteen."

"Keep up the good work," she said, nodding to the silence in the room and then vanishing.

We had one.

We had gone through only nine of over a hundred.

This really was hell. We just had to make sure we didn't miss anyone from this time so that we didn't repeat this hell into eternity.

No pressure.

CHAPTER TWELVE
The Swamp of People's Lives

WE MADE IT through the next nine without finding anyone from our time. Of that I was 100 percent sure. With Patty slowing down even more the moment that Screamer had touched each person, we were all digging into each person's life.

And there was a lot of it I flat didn't want to dig into.

One was a child molester that when we went over it with our pens and paper,

both Screamer and I made a note to look up to see if he was still alive.

Others had strange sexual habits that were not illegal, but made me look away. Others were buried in loneliness, others still were using gambling as a way to escape one ugly thing or another in their life. Of the nine, not a one of them was a happy person.

I'm not sure if that was a comment on slot players or just the luck of the draw.

As we finished with the third nine and came back to the present, Madge brought us all milkshakes and big baskets of hot fries. The vanilla milkshake tasted wonderful and the fries were perfect.

I didn't realize how much I needed both.

We again went over each name and it was number twenty-two that had come from today.

Penny Smith was her name. She had been widowed the year before at the age of fifty-four and was using gambling with slots to take her mind off her sorrow of losing the man of her life to cancer. I had no idea what she had done when she discovered she was trapped in the past, and I wasn't sure I wanted to know.

Screamer said the same thing.

Patty and Sherri said nothing.

Ben seemed to never make a comment on the people whose privacy we were invading.

So we had two after going through twenty-seven people.

We found the next one from this time two groups of nine later. Number forty-two.

She was a widower at thirty-five because her husband had been murdered. Actually, it was clear in her mind that she had murdered him for having an affair on her.

She had gotten all his money, played the grieving widow for a year or so, and then moved to Vegas last year.

"We'll deal with her after all this is settled," Screamer said, smiling at me.

I had no doubt he and the police would deal with her just fine. But after seeing the inside of that woman's evil mind, I wanted to help, or at least watch the police arrest her. She had already been plotting on finding her next rich husband when we stranded her in the past.

Beside me, Patty shuddered. "There is true evil out there, isn't there?"

I touched her arm and gave her energy to go on.

She smiled at me and said, "Thanks. Not so sure how I got so lucky to find someone like you."

"Raspberry shampoo," I said.

Screamer snorted and Patty had the decency to blush.

I had a clear memory of being in lust with Patty right from the first time I saw her. But all these trips into the memories of that time were making the fact that I really had fantasies about her and her raspberry soap in a shower, long before we climbed into that first shower together.

I loved that soap then and now.

"Clear your mind, mister," she said, softly smacking my arm. "We have work to do."

And I tried, I really did. But it's raspberry shampoo, after all.

CHAPTER THIRTEEN
Just One Small Problem Named Hank

WE GOT THROUGH all of the people we rescued from the ghost slots and found eleven.

We were all convinced there were only the eleven. I'm not a betting man, but I would have bet that was it. Of

Some Classic Jukebox Stories
Available at your favorite booksellers.

course, we were betting our entire lives and all the lives in this timeline that we were right.

We were also all exhausted, completely and totally.

"All right, Stan," I said into the air and he appeared.

"Ready for the Bookkeeper's list?" he asked.

"We are," I said.

Lady Luck appeared and sat at the end of the table with Stan. She grabbed one of the cold fries and started biting on it.

I had a master list in front of me and Patty, so I said, "Read off your names."

Lady Luck seemed to have a list as well and was following along.

He did, and I put a check beside each name that agreed with our list.

And then he read the name Hank Carson.

No Hank Carson on our list.

We all looked up at him and he clearly read our expressions.

"Oh, oh," he said.

"Hank's on my list as well," Lady Luck said. "Kronos and I put it together from studying time stream shifts over the last ten years."

I looked at Patty, then at Ben.

"No Hank Carson came out of the machine," I said.

Stan nodded and went on with the list. Everything agreed except that one name.

"How many people are between the two names we agree on?" Stan asked.

"Thirteen," Ben said. "Is Hank Carson a man or a woman?"

"A man," Lady Luck said.

"Then only four men are candidates," he said.

I flipped back through my notes to the four he was talking about and looked at them again.

All five of us did the same. I remembered all four men clearly. All had clearly been from 2004.

After a moment I looked up. "We go back. Look for anything out of place, dig deeper into these four."

Screamer nodded and said, "Ready."

Sherri took Ben's hand, Patty put her hand on my leg.

I took Screamer's hand and Sherri touched his leg.

And once again we were back in front of those damn evil machines.

Concentrate, Ben thought at us.

The first man came out and Screamer pushed him aside. But as he did, Patty slowed down time and we all dove into the poor man's mind.

After what seemed like far too long inside a stranger's head and looking into his very personal thoughts and actions, Screamer thought to us, *He's clean.*

We went on to the next guy.

Same.

And the next guy.

Same.

And the final guy.

Same.

There was no doubt, all four of them were taken by the slots in 2004.

Screamer broke the connection and we all turned to look at Stan and Lady Luck.

"No Hank Carson?" Stan asked.

"No Hank Carson," I said.

"Damn it," Lady Luck said again as she stood. "What the hell is going on here?"

And with that she vanished.

"I hate it when Mom swears," Sherri said, shaking her head and looking at her notes. "Things tend to turn ugly when that happens."

I could sure understand that. Never wanted to get Lady Luck mad. Something about that just seemed really, really dangerous.

I looked over at Stan. "How many hours do we have left?"

"Ten," he said.

Ten hours to save everyone in the world from being trapped in a nasty time loop. No wonder it was strictly against the rules to time travel. This kind of stuff was just far, far too dangerous.

CHAPTER FOURTEEN
Looking for Hank in All the Wrong Places

THE MOMENT Lady Luck vanished, Stan got back onto the phone with the Bookkeeper and gave him the name of Hank Carson. "We need every detail about the guy, right down to his shoe size," Stan said.

He listened to the Bookkeeper say something for a moment, nodded and then hung up without saying another word.

"He'll have it all within a half hour," Stan said, sitting back down at the table.

Around us the sky was starting to darken and now the planes coming into the airport had lights on. Pretty soon, stretched out below my invisible floating office, the lights of Las Vegas would be on and in full glory. Normally, I loved looking at those lights from here, but right now I didn't feel much like looking at anything except my hands.

Finally, I took a deep breath, put my hand on Patty's arm, and looked at the group. "So if we didn't pull Hank Carson out of that machine, why are both Kronos and the Bookkeeper showing that he

was there and part of what caused this alternate timeline?"

I looked around at my team. "I'm open for theories or even wild speculation."

Screamer shrugged. "He got with one of the survivors and discovered information about the future and used it, thus causing Kronos and the Bookkeeper both to pick up the disruptions he caused."

I nodded. I had figured as much. So if we pulled the others from the past and brought them back to the present, they would never hook up with Hank and thus that would take care of him.

But that was taking a horrible gamble I didn't want to take.

And it honestly didn't feel right to me. My little voice I trusted in poker said that wasn't the right way to go.

"A second option," Sherri said, "is that he's some sort of time traveler that used the trips by the Slots of Saturn to cover his tracks from Kronos."

"There are time travelers?" I asked, feeling stunned.

Sherri nodded. "Mostly from the distant future, but Kronos and his teams keep them out of these times for just this reason."

I glanced at Stan and he was nodding.

"If that's the case, it's out of our hands," I said.

Everyone around the table agreed. If that was the case, that was a problem for Kronos and Laverne.

I looked at everyone. "Any more options, suggestions, or just flat wild theories?"

"The first one seems the most logical," Ben said.

"But that seems like something that Kronos and the Bookkeeper would have taken into account," I said. "All of these people will have talked to some people at one point or another."

"I agree," Screamer said.

"There's something we're missing," I said.

So once again we all sat there in silence.

At that moment, Madge appeared from the diner with a tray of milkshakes. "I can hear all of you thinking clear downstairs," she said, "so thought I would bring some thinking food."

She also had a couple of baskets of hot fries.

I watched as Patty took one, then dropped it and sucked on her thumb.

"Hot out of the fryer," Madge said. "Sorry, should have warned you."

Something just dinged at me really hard.

It was that poker sense of mine that dinged like a little alarm bell to tell me I was missing a detail that was right in front of me.

Patty inspected her thumb for a moment, then put it against the cold glass of the vanilla milkshake in front of us.

Again the little dinger in my head dinged again, like an annoying timer I needed to shut off but couldn't find.

Then it dawned on me what I was seeing.

Patty's thumb.

Hitchhiker.

Someone hadn't been taken inside the slot machines, but had hitchhiked back in time on them.

"Thank you, Madge," I said, sucking on the milkshake so hard it gave me an ice cream headache. "You gave us the answer."

"I did?" she asked, looking puzzled and everyone else looked at me in the same way.

"Patty," I said, "show everyone your burnt thumb."

"It's not really burnt," she said.

"Show them," I said, smiling at her.

She did.

"Now, with your thumb sticking out, make a fist."

She did.

"Of course," Stan said, laughing. "Damn it, Poker Boy, how do you make these weird connections?"

"What connections?" Screamer asked. "Missed me."

Patty was smiling at me and as she did, she stuck out her thumb again over the middle of the table, moving it from left to right as she said, "Going my way, mister?"

"Hitchhiker?" Screamer asked.

Sherri laughed and Ben just nodded.

"We know who we got out of the machine," I said.

"Not who rode on the back of the machine into the past," Stan said.

"Exactly," I said. "I know I never thought of looking around behind those machines."

"I didn't either," Patty said.

"But we have one problem," Stan said. "We don't know exactly when he took that trip back. He wasn't in any of the police reports of those rescued."

"So he went back with one of the first ones," Patty said, "and when the machine jumped again, he got out of the warehouse."

I could feel my stomach tightening up again. Those machines had been operating for almost a week before we got to the warehouse. Hank could have found himself in that warehouse at any point over that week and we wouldn't know when.

Ben looked at me and said, "We have only ten hours to figure out when he arrived there and get him before he gets out of that warehouse. And then get the other eleven back to our time as well."

"If that is how he got back there," Screamer said. "Remember, our first option is the most logical, that he met someone from the future and was influenced by them."

I shook my head. "That doesn't feel right. The Bookkeeper would have spotted that. No, I think Hank rode along without meaning to. Not sure why I know that, but just a sense. Now we just have to figure out how."

And with that, again the silence filled the booth and my office overlooking the beautiful city of Las Vegas as the sun slowly set over the western hills.

CHAPTER FIFTEEN
Once More into the Nightmare

"So how do we find out when he rode back on the machines?" Sherri asked.

I looked at her and then asked the next logical question. "How could someone ride along and not be in the machine?"

"Touching it from the back," Screamer said.

Beside me, Patty shook her head. "Slot machines in this modern time are almost impossible to get close to from the back, unless he was a maintenance worker or a slot tech. Sitting in one of the other chairs is the most logical thing to have happened."

I couldn't believe I had forgotten that the machine was actually three slot machines.

With three wooden chairs attached.

It was only the machine on the right side that had come alive and had taken all our focus, but the other two machines rode along because it was a three-machine unit.

"Of course," I said. "We go back again, focus only on the moment the person from this time period was pulled into the machine to see if anyone was sitting next to them."

"And once we spot him," Screamer said, "we'll have a general timeline."

"I agree," Ben said. "We can figure out exactly when the two people on either side from that time were pulled through. That should narrow the time down to a few hours."

"So we go back to the nightmare and inside the heads of the eleven people taken from this time."

Everyone nodded. But clearly none of them were any happier with the idea than I was.

"I'll tell Lady Luck what you are doing," Stan said, and vanished.

Screamer was still sitting in the middle, with Patty on one side and me on the other.

"One more time?" I asked.

"Do we have a choice?" Screamer asked.

"Not that I can think of," I said.

"Then one more time."

Again, we scooted together in the booth and all touched so that our minds were all hooked up.

I thought at everyone, *Focus at the first person from our time and the moment they were at the machine.*

We did just that.

And once again I was back in that warehouse, with the feeling of panic and fear crawling all over me like a nest of spiders. Sherri instantly calmed all of us down.

Thanks, Patti thought.

Again, with Sherri keeping us calm, I could actually think and get out of the panic I felt back ten years ago as we fought to save over a hundred people from those machines.

We were again in slow motion as Patty had slowed time down, and we were back in our own memories. Then the woman from our time slowly appeared, being spit out by the machine like a bad coin, and Screamer pushed her out of the chair.

Patty slowed the moment down even more so that we could see into the poor woman's mind and see if there happened to be anyone around her that she noticed when she sat at the slots.

No one.

She was the only one in the chairs when the machine took her, and there was no way anyone could get in behind the old slots either, since they were against a wall.

One down, I thought at everyone.

We went through three more people from our time before we found what we were looking for.

The man named Jeffrey Johns, number sixty-four in the list of people we had rescued from the machine. He had just sat down in the chair when the machine was back at Binion's in this time period.

Suddenly, beside him, another man slid into the left seat.

There was a clear thought of annoyance from Jeffrey because he had been thinking of playing all three slot machines at the same time. Then he was pulled into the machine and into the past.

I got a clear image of the man who sat down in the left chair. Balding head, overweight, Bermuda shorts, and a Hawaiian shirt of loud blues and oranges.

I have a hunch that's him, I thought at everyone.

We check all eleven, Ben thought clearly.

I agreed.

And we did, and that was the only hitchhiker we found from our time back into the past.

Screamer cut the connection and we all moved back into our positions at the booth. Stan had returned and he and Madge were there, waiting for us to return from the nightmare of the past that we had been exploring in our minds.

"We found him," I said, smiling.

Ben quickly looked through his notes. "He arrived in 2004 somewhere in an eight-hour-period of time."

"Great job," Stan said. "Poker Boy, call the Bookkeeper and see if he can narrow the time down some. I'll tell Lady Luck so she can work with Kronos."

Then he vanished.

I grabbed my phone and quickly told the Bookkeeper what we had found and he said simply, "I'll be back with you in twenty minutes."

"So how long did that take?" I asked.

I was known for not wearing a watch or being able to keep track of time that well. Yet in this countdown, we had to keep track.

"We have just under nine hours to stop the time loop from setting," Ben said.

My heart sank and I could feel what energy I had left sort of draining out of me. And as it did, it was as if I could suddenly hear a huge clock ticking.

Just ticking in the distance.

On and on and on.

Slowly getting louder and taunting me with every tick of the clock.

To be continued...

Now Available
from all your favorite booksellers in trade paper and electronic editions.

FANTASY

USA TODAY BESTSELLING AUTHOR
DEAN WESLEY SMITH

THE **SLOTS** OF **SATURN**

A POKER BOY NOVEL

Dean Wesley **Smith**

USA Today Bestselling Writer

Living Forever In Ice
Makes Nostalgia
Very Deadly

NOSTALGIA 101

One thousand years in the future, humans live very long lives in domes on the frozen surface. Boredom never poses a threat, but nostalgia does.

When it becomes deadly to focus on the past, teaching nostalgia solves the problem.

USA Today *bestselling writer Dean Wesley Smith takes a peak into the final exam of the class called Nostagia 101.*

"Nostalgia 101" was first published in 2001 in a slightly different form in Millennium 3001 *from DAW Books, edited by Marin H. Greenburg and Russell Davis.*

NOSTALGIA 101

ONE

WE LEFT THE DOMED CITY of Portland through the western gate, moving along the old Columbia River bed. Centuries ago, ice had jammed up the Columbia Gorge to the east of Portland, forming an ice field that stretched for a thousand kilometers. Nothing existed in, on, or under that ice field. It moved and shifted too much to be safe.

The wind bit at my shield-protected face, cutting through even my special thermal suit. An unprotected human body in this cold would die in less than a minute. A bad suit tear could kill if not fixed quickly enough.

The danger of being out of the dome always excited me, got my heart racing, made all the research and work leading up to this trip worth it. I loved going out of the domes, had since I was a kid a few hundred years before. Just as everyone did when leaving a dome directly into the snow, we got the standard lecture of too much time in the cold can kill, too much time free-breathing can kill, and on and on. Exciting stuff the first time, the two hundredth time, it was real boring.

"Rees, can you hear me, son?" the Professor asked through the com-link in my ear. "Stay to the right and in the river basin."

I was leading, Lara followed me, then Torman, then Jeanette, then the Professor. Five sleds, five self-contained living units if they had to be. We didn't plan on being out long enough to use those features.

"Will do, sir," I said.

I always addressed Professor Barren Stanton as sir. I never called him by name. I didn't feel I had the right to call a man almost a thousand years old by his name. Besides, he insisted he be called Professor or sir and who was I to argue?

As I accelerated away from the base of the dome, the wind force field on the front of the hoversled rose into place, blocking any blowing snow and ice from hitting my environmental suit. I eased the sled up to one hundred and twenty and settled there, the agreed-upon speed.

The snow-covered terrain sped past in a blur. There was really nothing to see, since the ice and snow had killed everything hundreds of years ago. I clicked on the hoversled autopilot controls and sat back, adjusting the controls only when I thought the computer needed the help to make a bend in the riverbed.

Thankfully, mankind had discovered the cooling of the sun hundreds of years before it happened and had prepared, after a period of panic and religious insanity. As the sun's cooling phase started, some people had left the planet, moving into self-sustaining stations closer to the sun. Some day I hoped to visit one of those stations on vacation from my job managing a restaurant. I just hadn't had the chance yet.

Other groups had built large spaceships, Generation Ships as they were called, and simply headed off slowly toward other stars in search of a new home, one that wasn't about to be covered in ice. Nothing had been heard from those ships in hundreds of years. Nothing was expected for hundreds more.

Most of the population of Earth had decided to stay and wait the sun's cooling phase out. With the help of nanites back in the early twenty-first century, humans now lived thousands of years, maybe longer. No one was sure, since only a thousand years had passed. With nanites, humans had time to wait for the melt. Scientists predicted the sun would start into a heat-up cycle in less than five hundred years. I wouldn't even be as old as the professor by then.

TWO

IT TOOK just over an hour for us to reach the frozen Pacific. Millions and millions of humans lived under the frozen oceans of the planet, in the depths near thermal trenches, in domes that hugged the ocean floors like ancient coral. I had been into an ocean dome twice and both times didn't like the damp feel and the darkness that seemed to creep in from all sides.

I liked surface domes, with the intense white of the snow and the constant of the deep blue sky in the day and star fields at night. Surface domes were kept clear, ocean domes opaque. I loved the openness, the whiteness of everything. I had been born in the Reno dome three years short of two hundred years ago. I sure didn't feel that old, especially around the Professor. Nevertheless, on my two hundredth birthday, I planned on closing the restaurant and throwing a private birthday party for myself. I always figured that starting a person's third century of living should be celebrated and I planned on doing just that.

How could anyone get anything done in a short seventy to one hundred years of living? I worked full time, sure, had had a couple of marriage contracts with women, but basically, I was still in school, and would be off and on for another thirty years. Only after finishing all my classes would I feel really ready to contribute to society.

This class had become a prerequisite to any professional jobs above waiting tables. Nostalgia 101. The problem with living a long time had not been boredom, as many had predicted, but nostalgia.

Dreams and thoughts of a time that seemed better, seemed more comfortable, seemed easier, often pulled a normally productive human down to a complete standstill. Or worse, it made them collectors of things from the long dead past. Collectors wasted dome space, inflated prices of worthless things, and basically contributed nothing to the forward progress of society.

Five hundred years ago, nostalgia had become such a debilitating factor in society that suicide became the main cause of death above accidents. Classes were mandated to cure the problem. Hospitals were set up to treat the worst inflicted. Living basically forever was a wonderful thing, as long as you remained looking into the promise of the future.

For me, the dreaded nostalgia so far hadn't become a factor. I liked new everything, didn't collect anything, and didn't even much like old movies. I was happy with my life now, but even still, I had to take the class, prepare myself for the time when nostalgia might take me over.

I turned south along the old Pacific shoreline and kicked the speed up to two hundred kilometers per hour, skimming over the frozen ocean surface. The others followed at safe distances.

I couldn't imagine being born into a pre-dome life, back before nanites. But as the professor said, this expedition was going to help me with that lack of understanding. We were in search of a home he had known existed when he was born. A cave home that had survived the big Pacific fault quake of 2067. He claimed that after the quake, the house had been closed down and sealed by its owners. It might be possible that artifacts from over a thousand years ago were still in that home.

The problem was, of course, finding it under the hundreds of feet of snow and ice, using only records from three coastline shifts before the freeze. The five of us had signed up for this class with the professor four years ago. We had traveled the world searching through ancient stored information and books, arguing, learning, pinpointing what we thought might be the exact location of the home.

One of the main things I had learned in the process was that looking into the past was a very time-consuming and expensive thing to do. Why anyone would do it as a hobby was beyond me. It had to be a sickness, of that I was sure.

Now, we were approaching the agreed-upon site, the one place all our research led us to believe we might find the old building and thus discover something about ourselves, human history, and more importantly, nostalgia.

THREE

MY SCREENS showed I had almost reached our destination.

I slowed and turned the sled toward the slopes and ice cliffs that indicated the old coastline. Hundreds of thousands of people had lived along this ocean's shores before the freeze. I had seen images of these places, old movies of walking on sandy beaches. I just couldn't imagine it. My entire life had been in the comforts of the domes and the white nothingness of the snow.

I eased my sled up onto a slight incline and then stopped when my computer told me I had arrived at the right coordinates. I did a quick sounding of the slopes and cliffs above me, checking for any chances of ice slides, then signaled the all clear.

"Well done, son," Professor Stanton said to me as he pulled up his sled beside the rest of ours. I nodded and stayed on my sled. I could monitor all the progress of the search from there on the sled's screens.

Torman and Lara already had out their equipment and were scanning the ice field below us. They looked almost identical in their environmental suits and masks. We all looked the same, even the Professor.

"There's something down there," Lara said, her voice level.

I could feel the excitement of a possible find surge through me. Could we get lucky enough to actually find the old cave house so quickly?

I watched the information come over my screens. The details were correct, the shape of the opening that we had trained to look for, the age of the blockage in the cave mouth. All fit. Thirty-six meters down.

But something about the ice and snow around it didn't seem right. I couldn't put my finger on exactly what it was.

"We have found it," Professor Stanton said, his voice flat as always. "Jeanette, are you ready?"

"I am, Professor," she said.

I could hear the excitement in her voice. She was the youngest of the four of us at just under one hundred and fifty. Like me, her job in the Portland dome was to manage a restaurant. I would have been interested in a contracted relationship with her if she hadn't already been in contract with another woman. And she seemed neutral to me, so I never pushed anything.

"Then, open us a path to the cave home."

Jeanette moved her sled back away from the hill, then watching her screens instead of the white in front of her, she turned on her heat drill attached to the front of her sled.

I watched as the drill melted the ice, fusing it into a ten meter in diameter tunnel down toward the cliff house.

The tunnel formed very quickly, almost too quickly.

I ran a few non-connected scans of the snow and area we were in. I could see traces of the remains of other closed-up tunnels.

Many others.

Maybe thousands.

Jeanette drilled down right along the path of a former tunnel, which caused her much easier digging.

I said nothing about my findings, but I instantly lost the excitement I had been feeling about the find.

Excitement that Professor Stanton had warned me to contain.

He had said, "From this excitement comes nostalgia, and from nostalgia comes death. As a society, we must never look back. We must always look to the future. It is in the future that the true excitement lays."

Realizing that this wasn't an original find, that we were only going over the same stuff a hundred or thousand classes before us had gone over, made the professor's point very clearly.

Finally, Jeanette reached the mouth of the cave and shut off the tunneling device.

Professor Stanton climbed off his sled for the first time and using hover pads on his feet, moved to the mouth of the tunnel. "Shall we take a look at the past?" he said.

I wondered if he said the exact same thing to every class he taught. More than likely, he did. I didn't know if I should be angry at the years we had spent researching to find this place. I wasn't sure of the point of that part of the lesson.

I sat there as the others went to join the Professor.

"Are you coming, son?" he asked after a moment.

"Wouldn't it just be easier to look at the images recorded by earlier classes?"

The others spun to look at me through their environmental visors, but the Professor just nodded. "Yes, it would be, Rees. But that's not the point of this class, is it?"

"I'd be very interested in what *exactly* the point might be," I said.

"To give each and every one of you an understanding of nostalgia. That was in the course description. I'm sure you read it."

"By going to an old site where hundreds, maybe thousands have been before?"

"Of course," the Professor said. "History is where people have been before. Did you expect anything different?"

I started to say something, then realized he was right.

He went on. "Nostalgia is the disease that makes us continually want to be where others have been before, where we have been before."

"And what's the point of wanting that?" Jeanette asked.

"There is no point," the Professor said. "True excitement is always the unknown ahead. Torman, Lara, you saw in your scans that there had been many tunnels here before us."

"We did," Lara said.

Torman nodded.

"How did you feel?" the Professor asked.

"Disappointed," Lara said.

"Tricked," Torman said.

"And you, Jeanette, you saw it as well. How did you feel?"

"The same," she said, nodding.

"Yet, for the last few years, our mission in this class was to find this cave house in which people had lived, where people had been before. What is the difference that others had visited this site in the last hundred years, or a thousand years ago when it was built?"

I was starting to see his point. "The search for anything in the past is always the search for where someone else has been."

"Exactly, son," Professor Stanton said.

"But no one has been to tomorrow yet," Jeanette.

Professor Stanton nodded. "Now are you starting to understand why nostalgia is so dangerous? You just spent almost four years of your time to discover a place that others had been to, that others had lived in. Couldn't your time and money have been spent so much more constructively?"

I nodded, as did the others. Point made.

"So," Professor Stanton said, indicating the tunnel "anyone want to take a look at the past?"

"Why bother those who are dead and buried?" Jeanette said.

We all agreed with her and she closed up the shaft so that the next class might have its object lesson.

"Come in for one final discussion next week," Professor Stanton said. "I can safely say, you all passed with top marks."

After a few minutes, I turned my sled back north up the coastline, setting the speed at two hundred kilometers per hour. I had to admit, I was glad we hadn't wasted any more time going down that hole. It would be nice to get back in the dome, maybe check in with the restaurant and see how the dinner rush was doing.

And it felt very good passing this class. Now, I could sign up for my next class. "The Proper Use of Nanites in a Sexual Act."

That promised to be very informative.

~

DEAD MONEY could be the start of a new thriller genre— the political poker thriller.

—*Sheldon McArthur,*
former owner of
Mysterious Books in Los Angeles

Available Now
**from all your favorite booksellers
in trade paper and electronic editions.**

Now Available
from all your favorite booksellers
in trade paper and electronic editions.

DEAN WESLEY
SMITH

USA Today BESTSELLING AUTHOR

Morning

Song

A SEEDERS UNIVERSE NOVEL

Dean Wesley Smith

USA Today Bestselling Writer

She Arrived Without a Song

Without a Song

A Jukebox Story

Stout, the owner of the Garden Lounge, always thought he could control the time machine disguised as a jukebox by keeping it unplugged.

Then one day the jukebox started up without power and a visitor from the future asked a very important favor.

A favor that would not only save lives, but maybe everyone.

SHE ARRIVED WITHOUT A SONG
A Jukebox Story

ONE

"STOUT!"

The shout wasn't really something I paid much attention to. I was standing with my back to the bar working on my bar order that needed to be done by three in the afternoon or the four regulars behind me weren't going to be drinking this weekend.

"Stout! You had better turn around real quick!"

That was Big Carl's voice and in all the years he had been coming into the Garden Lounge, I had never heard him raise his voice until now.

I spun around to find all four regulars turned and staring to my left. And they all looked shocked.

Big Carl, the farthest down the bar to the right looked almost panicked.

Fred and Billy, both retired older men in for an afternoon "bracer" as Fred liked to call his drink, looked like they had seen a ghost.

Richard, my friend who sometimes helped me out behind the bar when I needed a break was on the right and leaning back as if he was trying to move away from something that might bite him.

It took me a moment to see what they were staring at. Then it hit me like a hammer and I had to catch myself against the back bar.

The jukebox was on!

That jukebox was never to be plugged in or turned on unless I did it. And everyone knew that. At least everyone sitting at the bar at the moment and there was no one else in the bar on this sunny July afternoon. Even in the faint light of some of the booths, I knew no one else was in here. In the summer, when someone came in or left, the bright sunshine from outside lit up the normally fairly dark Garden Lounge like the insides of a spotlight.

And every time a person came in they had to stop, let the door close, and then let their eyes adjust before moving.

The jukebox was on.

Not possible.

For a second I thought it was one of my regulars playing a joke on me, but they all looked as shocked as I felt and they knew I wouldn't consider anyone messing with the jukebox any kind of joke at all.

So I clicked off the stereo behind the bar and eased toward where the old Wurlitzer jukebox sat tucked behind a planter off the open end of the bar.

It was out of sight from most of the tables in the bar and on busy nights I just covered it with an old gray cloth to keep anyone from deciding to plug it in and play a song when I wasn't looking.

That old jukebox was very special. It could take a person back to the actual memory of the song being played. And the person, while there, while the song was playing, could change the memory, their own history if they wanted.

And that made the jukebox frighteningly dangerous. It only got turned on for the seven friends that knew about it on Christmas Eve every year, friends who understood the danger of tinkering with their own past in the slightest.

But there the jukebox sat on this hot July afternoon, lights bright, the hum of whatever secret time travel device was inside it filling the now deadly silent bar.

I eased around and looked behind the jukebox.

"It's not plugged in," I said out loud, more to myself than the other four in the bar as I backed away.

"Not possible," Richard said softly. "That power is coming from somewhere."

At that moment the motor started to whir that brought up a record.

I wanted to just run for the street and the heat outside, but instead stumbled back behind the bar, too shocked to even think.

Somehow that jukebox, without power, was about to play a song. Not possible. It could take all of us out and back in time to memories we didn't want to go to.

Suddenly, I realized what I had to do and my mind broke free of the shock for the moment. In two steps I reached the drawer under the cash register and yanked it open. In the back was the box of high-grade earplugs clipped together in pairs. I yanked out a handful and scattered them in front of everyone along the bar, then grabbed two for myself.

"Quickly, get these in and think about a pleasant memory."

All of them moved as one, grabbing earplugs and stuffing them into place.

I did the same, moving back around the end of the bar to the jukebox to see which record the thing was going to play.

It picked the slot A-1, where I used to have the record that took me back to Jenny. I hadn't had that record in the jukebox for years, so the pick-up arm of the jukebox picked up nothing and moved toward the platter as I watched.

"It doesn't have a record!" I shouted so everyone could hear me over the earplugs.

But the machine kept pretending it did have a record, dropping the imaginary record on the turntable. A moment later it spun up and the playing arm moved into place, resting over the empty, spinning turntable like a record was actually there.

I had to be dreaming.

That was the answer. This had to be an ugly nightmare. I had come to respect the jukebox and whoever had built it. Time travel in any fashion was dangerous and I had had many nightmares about that machine as well.

But never one where the jukebox played without being plugged in.

That was always the control I had over the thing. No power, it didn't work.

Up until now.

TWO

THEN, as some imaginary song on an imaginary record started to play, there was a shimmering in front of the jukebox, or actually more accurately right over the jukebox, and the image of flowers and colors and bubbles appeared surrounding a beautiful woman.

She looked almost see-through and she was wearing what looked like sound-dampening headphones.

She smiled and started to speak, but I couldn't hear her because of the earplugs. She indicated I should take them out.

Trying to think of the best memory I could, I eased the plug out of my right ear.

There was no song. No music at all, just this image of a woman shimmering over the jukebox, sort of fading in and out.

"It's clear!" I shouted to the others and everyone pulled out their earplugs. They were all looking as stunned as I was feeling.

All of us had seen people disappear and then reappear as the jukebox took them back to a memory and then brought them back when the song ended. But only once before had a song brought a person to us.

And never had someone come to the jukebox without it being plugged in and with no actual song playing.

The woman floating over the jukebox smiled and the area around her sort of radiated the joy of her smile, the colors becoming brighter and the swirling lines moving faster.

She did not take off her headphones.

"Hi, Stout," she said, nodding to me.

I had never met her before that I could remember, and she was attractive enough I'm sure I would have remembered.

Then she turned to Richard and the look in her eyes changed slightly in a way I couldn't tell. "Thank you for giving me this chance. It looks like it worked, at least the first part of this."

I glanced around at my friend.

Richard just sat there, looking shocked, his mouth slightly open as he stared at the beautiful woman floating above the jukebox.

I finally managed to swallow, then through a very dry mouth asked the obvious first questions.

"Who are you and where are you coming from?"

I wanted to ask how, but figured I needed the first two questions answered first.

"My name is Donna Neff. I'm thirty-seven and you don't know me yet. I am coming back from a future I hope to change."

I nodded, tried to swallow again without much success. She was a young-looking thirty-seven.

She smiled and answered my next question. "I don't know how this is being done either. In the future Richard figures some of this sort of stuff out about this fantastic jukebox."

Again I glanced at my friend, but he wasn't moving. His gaze was just locked on the woman.

"The song is half over," she said, glancing down at the jukebox and where the arm was in its position on the imaginary record.

"What can we do to help you?" I asked. "And why should we?"

"The why is the easy part, sort of," she said. "To save the world, to put it bluntly."

I didn't like the sound of that, but I just let her go on. I didn't much like any of this at this point.

"Please don't ask me how I know, I just do, just as I know about this wonderful jukebox. Time travel is very possible, as you all know. My son Danny will invent a device when he is in college that will eventually solve a lot of the energy problems of the world. That's all I can say because it's pretty much all I know."

I nodded and glanced at the jukebox. Whatever song that had sent her was getting close to being over.

"Go on," I said.

"I am told that in about ten minutes a girlfriend and I will come through the front door of the Garden looking for a cool drink and you all will treat us wonderfully, since you are all great people. And we

will become regulars, using the Garden as a sanctuary away from our children and divorces and crummy ex-husbands."

"And you changed your past, right?" I asked. I knew the answer because she said that she had been told. She had gone through the jukebox at some point in the future and changed her past.

She nodded. "One Christmas, because I was slightly drunk and not really thinking, I went back through the jukebox and said something to my future and ex-husband on our first date."

"And you never got married and Danny was never born to save the world."

She nods. "That's what I am told by others from yet another future."

"You and Richard found me again, because I had never come into the Garden in my new life, and invited me back to the Garden and I met my old friend and she told me everything, since she was touching the Jukebox when I left."

I still didn't understand the part about her son inventing something in a future that no longer existed. How could anyone come back from that future, that timeline to tell her anything?

She smiled at Richard. "A while after you found me again, Richard, you got a visit from a son you had in my first world, our son, actually, a son that somehow crossed over timelines to warn us."

She smiled. "In the timeline I changed, you and I were talking about getting married and we had had a child. But you didn't remember it either because you hadn't been touching the jukebox when I screwed up."

As she started to fade, she glanced at me and then looked directly at Richard. "Please don't let that happen to my first son, and to our son. Don't ever let me go through the jukebox. Ever."

And then she was gone.

THREE

A MOMENT LATER the jukebox ran through the return routine, put the invisible record back in the A-1 slot and then went dark.

The quiet in the bar was so intense, it felt like my ears were ringing.

I forced myself to take a deep breath and move back behind the bar, staying a good distance away from the now clearly unplugged and powerless jukebox.

I was almost afraid to even look at Richard, but I did.

He sat there, mouth open, staring at the now dead jukebox.

"I've got to admit," Fred said as I clicked on the stereo to break the silence. "You sure know how to put on an afternoon's entertainment."

Everyone but Richard drank to that.

I stared at my old friend. He was in his early forties, had never been married, and didn't drink, although he used to. He was a plant manager by day and spent his evenings here in the Garden with friends sipping on orange juice and grenadine and helping me when I needed help. Sometimes, on long lunch breaks, like today, he came in to cool down. In the Garden we didn't call his drink a Shirley Temple, as they did in every other bar. We called them "A Richard," and Richard was proud of that fact.

I took my glass of fresh-brewed iced tea and leaned against the backbar, trying to put aside the shock and deal with what had just happened.

I was used to thinking about time travel over the last years of owning the Garden and that jukebox. And if we didn't welcome the women who were about to come in the door, we would feel a faint shimmering and we would never remember she had come to visit us.

I knew that for a fact. If we chased the two women away, we would have changed the future, the future where she and Richard meet and have a child. She would save her first son, but not Richard's son. If we chased the two women away we would kill the child who would grow up to understand time travel well enough to cross timelines.

Somehow we had to save both sons.

And I knew exactly what I had to do. What we all had to do. We had no choice.

And we had to do it quickly, before that door opened and let in the outside sun and heat and two women looking for a cool drink.

"Listen up!" I said, not shouting, but getting everyone to look up at me instantly, including Richard.

"That never happened," I said, pointing at the jukebox. "We never saw her, never heard what she had to say."

"But Stout," Fred said, "that would mean she would lose her son."

"No, it won't," I said. Then I turned to Richard. "You and I will never, ever allow her to go back through that jukebox. Ever. Once she learns about what the jukebox can do, we will just never let her travel in time."

Richard nodded. "At some point we'll have to tell her why."

"I'll leave that up to you," I said, smiling. "When the time is right."

He just shook his head, staring down at his drink.

I grabbed a pair of earplugs from the bar in front of Richard, quickly hooked them back together, then took a bar napkin and wrote in large black ink, "Donna."

Then with a tack I put the earplugs up on a post above and to the right of the cash register. "For the future," I said.

I turned back around to my four friends. "We can't tell a word of this to anyone. Not even the other regulars. This is a very, very important secret. Lives are at risk, maybe even the future of our world. Are we in agreement?"

All four of the regulars facing me across the Garden Lounge bar nodded, their expressions very serious and intent.

"Then pick up your glasses for a toast," I said as I grabbed my iced tea.

All four regulars did and I raised my glass upward. "To the different possible futures."

"To the futures," they all said and we all drank.

A moment later the front door opened, flooding into the Garden Lounge bright sunlight and warmth. And through the door walked two attractive women. One was a slightly-younger Donna Neff.

Again, my stomach sort of flipped over.

It hadn't been a dream and the secret we had all just agreed to keep really did have lives and worlds at stake.

"Not a word," I whispered just loud enough for the four at the bar to hear me.

They all nodded as they all turned toward the front door, clearly staring at the two women.

Both women stopped just inside the door as it closed, trying to look around as their eyes adjusted to the dim light.

"Put on your most charming smiles, gentlemen," I whispered again.

Then I motioned for Richard to scoot down two stools closer to the jukebox to allow room at the bar for the two women to sit.

Then I went around the bar with a wide smile to greet a woman I had just met a few minutes before.

"Welcome to the Garden Lounge. Your eyes will adjust in a moment."

Somehow I kept myself from saying, "Welcome back to the Garden Lounge."

But I did.

And that boded well for the future. Maybe a number of futures.

~

Some Classic Poker Boy Stories

Available at your favorite booksellers.

Now Available
from all your favorite booksellers in trade paper and electronic editions.

USA TODAY BESTSELLING AUTHOR
DEAN WESLEY
SMITH

HEAVEN PAINTED
as a poker chip

A GHOST OF A CHANCE NOVEL

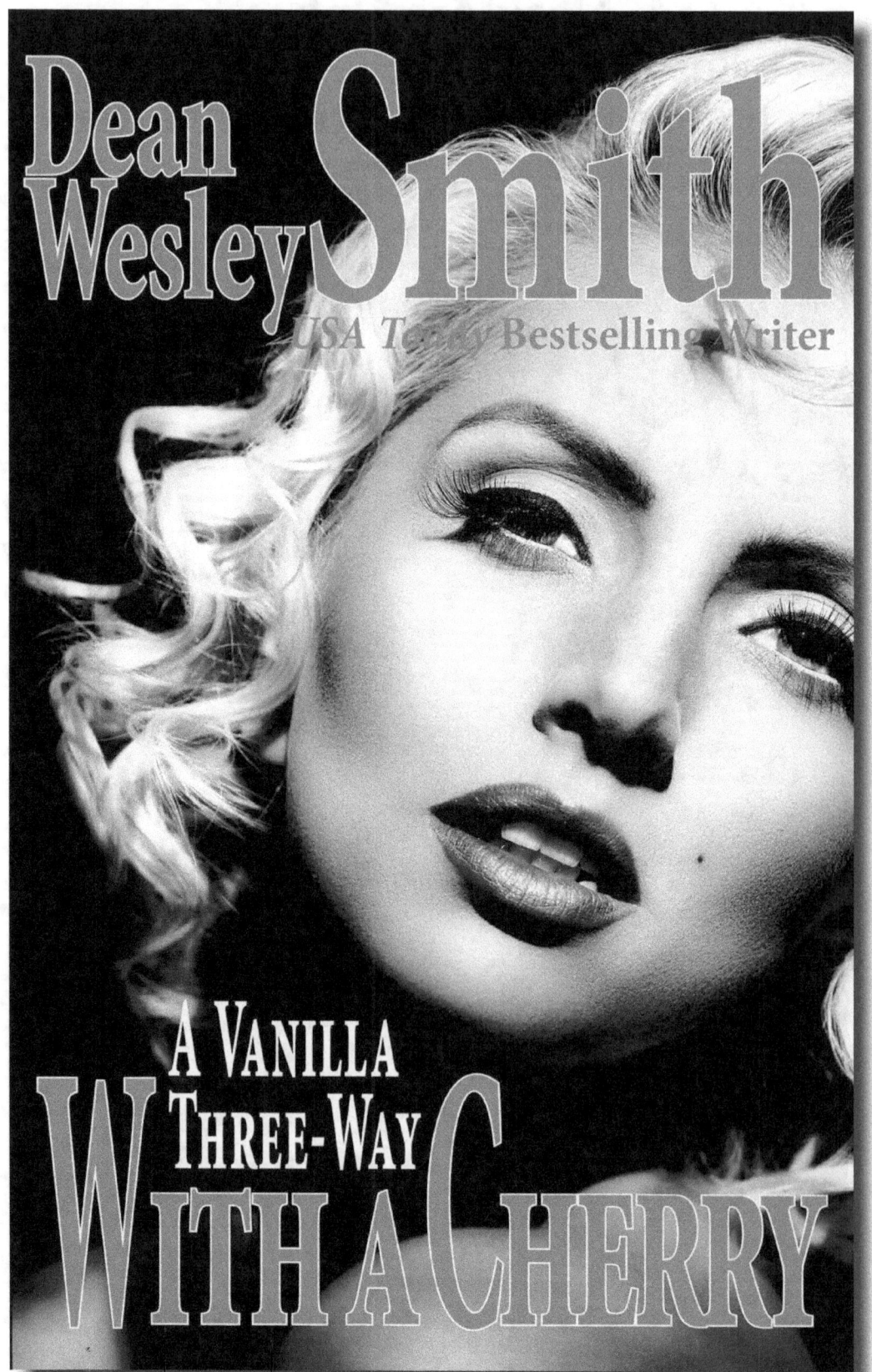

Dean Wesley Smith

USA Today Bestselling Writer

A VANILLA
THREE-WAY
WITH A CHERRY

When the ghost of Marilyn Monroe joins you and your girlfriend for a milkshake with a cherry on top, things change in a relationship, sometimes for the better.

Especially when your girlfriend thinks she just might be Norma Jean.

A VANILLA THREE-WAY WITH A CHERRY

ONE

Someone had hung a framed, black-and-white photo of Marilyn Monroe right over the diner's only urinal. The picture was about a quarter life-sized, which made her a *very* dominating presence. The bathroom was the standard restaurant bathroom, with a tile floor, metal stall, and painted walls. It was as clean as I had ever seen a bathroom, no graffiti anywhere.

Only Marilyn's picture.

In the photo Marilyn had turned her shoulders sideways, keeping her face straight and looking over her shoulder. She was wearing a low-cut black evening gown. Real low cut, actually, with the old fifties-style bra cups that looked so sharp they could poke out a guy's eye if he went in at the wrong angle.

The points on those breasts were right at head level as I stood at the urinal, and for half the piss I couldn't look at anything else.

Then I glanced up.

Marilyn's face was framed by light, almost angel-like. She stared down at me, sort of smiling, as if she had known when the picture was taken that some guy would be holding his dick while staring at her tits.

I almost couldn't finish the job I was there to do.

And, to be honest, after looking into Marilyn's eyes, I had trouble looking back at her breasts. It just didn't seem respectful, even though those points were right there in front of me, and she was long dead.

So I kept my neck cranked upward, staring at her perfect face, that I-know-what-you-are-doing-smile, those dark eyes. I have no idea how long I stood there, penis flapping in the air-conditioning, just staring at her. I don't even know what I was thinking. I had never been attracted to Marilyn before.

Finally, I realized I was finished and managed to pull away from the picture, get myself zipped up, hands washed, and headed out the door.

"You all right, baby doll?" Betty asked as I slid back into the booth, her gum popping as it often did when she was flustered. Clearly I had been in there with Marilyn for a long time.

Betty and I had been dating for five months, from the moment she had come into my garage to have her classic T-Bird's transmission fixed. Betty loved anything about the fifties. She kept her blonde hair in the old flipped up way, and often wore fifties-style blouses, poodle skirts, and shoes with white socks. When she dressed like that it made her look one hell of a lot younger than her twenty-eight years.

And hotter.

She also loved *Happy Days* on television, and any movie set in the fifties, no matter how stupid. I know, because we had watched a bunch of them.

This diner, "The Fifties Place," was her favorite restaurant, with its Elvis pictures on the wall, Wurlitzer bubble juke-box, and bright red vinyl booths. But tonight was the first time the Marilyn picture had been in the bathroom. I was pretty sure I would have noticed it before.

The diner seemed busier than it had been when I had gone into the bathroom. And the waitress had already brought us the vanilla milkshake we had ordered just as I left to pee.

What the hell had happened to the time? People had always said that Marilyn had a strange effect on men, but this was getting silly. It was just a damn picture.

I pulled my thoughts back out of the men's room and focused on the table in front of me and at the three milkshakes.

"Three?"

The servings in this place were so big, we usually ordered only one shake, and an extra glass to pour the rest of the shake out of the tin mixing cup. But this time we had three vanilla shakes on the table, all in the nifty glasses. The top of the tall, heavy, glasses was wider than the bottom, which tapered down to a glass base.

The waitress had added whipped cream to the top of all of them, and two of the shakes still had their red cherries perched on top. Only the cherry from the glass in front of Betty was missing. She loved the things, so I had no doubt that cherry had given its life over her thick, full lips.

"They needed the mixing cup," Betty said, "so the waitress just poured it all in glasses and gave us extra whipped cream."

I nodded, just staring at the three milkshakes. Maybe I should offer one to Marilyn.

Betty reached a hand forward and touched my arm. "Baby?"

I looked into her deep brown eyes and saw the worry there. I hadn't gotten past second base with her in six months, because, as she said, "Good girls don't do that sort of thing." Maybe if she thought I was sick or something, I might get a little nursing.

I instantly decided against that idea. Betty liked the image of guys from the fifties who were macho types, with their cigarettes rolled up in their tee-shirts, who fought over their girls at drive-in movies. Sick played no part in any image Betty had of me, I was sure of that.

"Fine," I said, smiling at her. "Just got staring at a new picture of Marilyn in the bathroom. Can't make myself believe how much you look like her."

Betty's face turned red and she smiled like I had just promised her a meeting with James Dean. "You really think so?"

"I sure do," I said, squeezing her hand. Actually, she sort of had a passing resemblance, but not much else. And her chest was half the size of Marilyn's, even without the pointed bra.

"You'll be my Joe DiMaggio?" she asked.

I wanted to say sure, if you let me slide into third base tonight, but instead just smiled and said, "Not sure if I can live up to that guy, but why not try?"

Betty loved humility in her man, and I could be as humble as was needed.

Suddenly her smiling face turned serious. "I've got an important question to ask you."

"Go ahead."

"Can I have your cherry?"

I almost blurted out, *I thought that I was supposed to ask that question.* Somehow I managed to say instead, "Which one?"

She laughed at that.

I slid the milkshake closest to me toward her and she took the red cherry,

holding it over her mouth for a moment before letting it go.

"I'll drink this one," I said, pulling back my cherry-less shake and putting a straw in it.

Then I put a straw in the third glass and slid it over to the seat beside me. "We'll save that one for Marilyn."

Betty smiled again. "You think she might join us?"

"Depends on if she can get out of the men's room in time," I said.

Betty actually laughed at the lame joke.

TWO

BETTY STARTED talking about a coming dance she wanted me to go to with her, and I got to nodding and thinking of Marilyn and that amazing look on her face.

Then the hamburgers came. I took the onions off of mine because Betty did the same, and sometime later tonight I hoped to be kissing Betty, and I didn't want onion breath spoiling the moment.

It was during my first bite that Betty said, "Not fair. You ate Marilyn's cherry."

I glanced at where the third shake sat. She was right, the cherry was gone, and the glass looked like someone had taken a good drink from it.

"I thought you didn't like the cherries," Betty said.

"I don't," I said, looking closer at Marilyn's shake without touching it. "The cherry must have just sunk when the whipped cream melted."

"Maybe Marilyn ate it."

Betty was looking at the shake and I had no doubt she was half serious. I just shook my head and went back to eating my burger.

But three bites later the level of the third milkshake was lower still, and there was no sign of the missing bright red cherry.

I hadn't touched the thing, and I knew Betty hadn't reached across the table and drank any of it. In fact, she was still staring at it, her eyes wide, her burger forgotten.

"What?" I asked.

"Marilyn," Betty whispered, not so much that she didn't want anyone to hear, but like she was in shock. Her face was white, her eyes round.

I glanced at the third milkshake on the table beside me. Again some more of it was gone. I was about to say something about the hole in the bottom of the glass when I caught a slight movement out of the corner of my eye.

Then I saw her.

Marilyn.

Sitting right *there* in the booth beside me, between me and the wall, leaning forward and sipping on the milkshake. She had on the same black, low-cut dress that she wore in the picture, so when she bent forward, everything about her sort of became skin. Beautiful, soft, pink skin. Not ghost-like at all.

Betty leaned over the table and grabbed my hand so hard I thought she was going to break it.

"You see her?" she whispered.

"Yeah," I said, not believing what my eyes were telling me.

Marilyn finished the shake, sucking the last of it from the straw with a slurping sound. Then she turned to me and Betty, putting a hand on my leg.

I kid you not, she touched me, softly, yet with overtones of sex like I had never felt before.

Betty kept hold of my hand.

Marilyn Monroe rubbed my leg.

"That was wonderful," Marilyn said, her voice almost a sigh, just like she had done in a bunch of her movies. "I haven't had a good vanilla milkshake in years. Thank you."

"My—my pleasure," I managed to say, even though my voice was screaming that I was dreaming, that I was still standing in the bathroom staring at her picture.

Marilyn squeezed my leg and laughed. Then she turned to Betty, leaving her hand on my thigh.

"Your boyfriend's right, Betty. You do look a little like me, in my Norma Jean days."

For a moment I thought Betty would just faint away. She clearly was having trouble breathing. Finally she managed to say, "Thanks."

Marilyn gave me one of her famous sideways glances that said more with one look than a million words could get across.

And then she went to rubbing my leg, up and down, up and down.

I was definitely more up than down at that moment.

I had to be dreaming.

I swore I was dreaming. But right at that moment, to be honest, I didn't care that I was or wasn't dreaming. I was going to enjoy it all.

Marilyn looked back at Betty. "You know the difference between Norma Jean and Marilyn?"

Betty managed to shake her head.

"Illusion," Marilyn said. "I'm an illusion, what men think they want in a woman. Marilyn is the sexual side of Norma Jean. Marilyn got famous, Norma Jean didn't."

Okay, now I knew this had gone too far. An illusion of Marilyn telling us she was an illusion. If it hadn't been for the hand stroking my leg, I would have laughed.

"Norma Jean was real," Marilyn said. "You're real, Betty. But you have a Marilyn side in you as well. Let it out to play, if you get my meaning."

Oh, god, I had died and gone to heaven. Marilyn Monroe was giving my girlfriend sex advice while giving me a hard on.

Marilyn smiled at Betty with that smile that only girls know the meaning of.

Betty smiled and nodded back at Marilyn.

I smiled as Marilyn's hand moved up my leg a little more.

"Thanks for the shake," Marilyn said.

Then with one last squeeze, very high up my thigh, she vanished.

THREE

SUDDENLY the noise from the diner came flooding back in, as if Marilyn being there had stopped it. A kid was crying two booths over, Buddy Holly doing his most famous song on the jukebox, and the waitress was talking to the people in the booth behind Betty.

It was as if the world had stopped for a few minutes, and I had been holding my breath.

I let out a deep sigh and looked around. It seemed no one had noticed Marilyn.

No one but me and Betty.

And my dick. It had most definitely noticed Marilyn's hand rubbing my leg.

Betty was still just sitting there, staring at where Marilyn had been, holding

my hand across the table as if she was about to slip over the edge of a cliff.

Finally, as someone knocked over a glass of water three booths over, I asked, "You all right?"

Betty took a moment, then with what looked like a force of will, pulled her gaze from where Marilyn had been and looked into my eyes.

"Did that just happen?"

"I'm not sure what just happened." I pointed at the empty milkshake glass. "But someone drank that thing."

Betty nodded, staring at the empty place beside me. Then she said softly, "Marilyn."

"One hell of an illusion," I said.

"Maybe," Betty said. "Maybe not."

We both sat there for a moment in silence, Betty still holding my hand. Then suddenly she said, "I want to see that picture in the bathroom." She stood and pulled me up behind her.

"In the men's room?" I asked. Betty had always struck me as the biggest prude to live in the new century. Imagining her going into a men's room just didn't seem possible.

"You make sure no one's in there first," Betty said.

We moved over to the door of the men's room and I poked my head inside. "Anyone in here?"

My voice echoed, so I turned to Betty and said, "Clear."

Betty pushed past me and stopped in the very center of the bathroom, with me still standing holding the door open.

"Where is it?" she asked.

"Over the urinal," I said, but the moment I said that I knew the picture, just like the Marilyn beside me in the booth, was gone. There was no way Betty would have missed seeing that picture.

I let the door close and moved to stand beside her, staring at the blank wall.

"It was right there," I said. "Honest."

Betty took my hand and laughed. "I know it was."

As she pulled me out of the men's room and we headed back to the table, the waitress gave us a dirty look. All I could do was shrug.

We finished our burgers and shakes, talking about Marilyn and what she had said, as if it really hadn't been an illusion, that she had just joined us from the land of the dead to share a vanilla milkshake.

After I had paid the bill, we left all three empty milkshake glasses together, touching in the center of the table, straws bent outward in three different directions.

And that night, back at my apartment, the Betty I had known for six months added a Marilyn side to her personality.

I have no idea if it was an illusion or not, but to be honest, I didn't care.

#1... October 2013

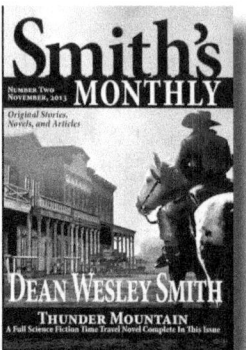

#2... November 2013

#3... December 2013

#4... January 2014

#5... February 2014

#6... March 2014

#7... April 2014

#8... May 2014

#9... June 2014

#10... July 2014

#11... August 2014

#12...September 2014

The Third Seeders Universe Novel
now available from all your favorite booksellers in trade paper and electronic.

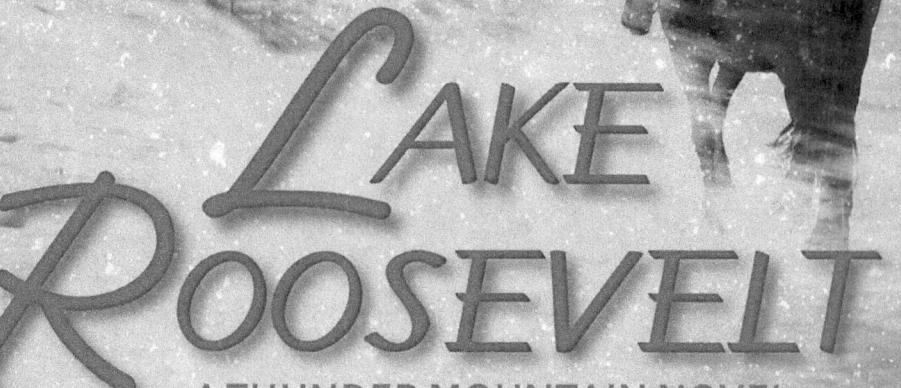

DEAN WESLEY SMITH

USA Today Bestselling Author

Lake Roosevelt

A Thunder Mountain Novel

In a small diner on the Oregon Coast, Kelli Rae meets a handsome man named Jesse Parks. Turns out she had seen him in a picture taken in an old mining town in Idaho over a hundred years before.

And even worse, he had been following her.

A time-travel adventure in the popular Thunder Mountain series that promises to change everything about the series.

LAKE ROOSEVELT
A Thunder Mountain Novel

This book is dedicated to Kris, who loves me enough to have gone with me into the remote lake once. Once was enough. Thanks.

AUTHOR'S NOTE

The town of Roosevelt existed. And it was actually destroyed by a mudslide that filled the valley and formed Lake Roosevelt over the top of the mining town.

I want to thank Bobby Young for helping me get to the remote lake the first time almost forty years ago now. Standing on the shores of Roosevelt Lake and staring down into the waters at the remains of the town of Roosevelt is a very strange experience that is very difficult to forget.

PART ONE
A Really Bad Picture

CHAPTER ONE

July 14th, 2016
Oregon Coast

WHEN A BESTSELLING historical crime writer sees a ghost, it's a bad, bad sign.

Kelli Rae had no idea why a ghost would haunt her, especially in the Whale Port Diner on the Oregon Coast.

Coming north along the winding highway, the Whale Port Diner had looked clean and funky and just the type of place that might serve a great chicken fried steak lunch. A girl's juices could really get moving over a good chicken fried steak with thick white gravy with just enough pepper to give it a bite.

Add yellow corn near the white gravy and you have heaven built right into a small-town diner.

She had wheeled her little blue two-door Mercedes into the small empty gravel parking lot and climbed out into the fantastic smell of ocean and beach. Two blocks down the hill below the two-lane highway, the surf pounded the rocks and sand, the sound so loud it almost covered up the noise from the few passing cars.

It was just after four in the afternoon and the sun was still high in the sky, but the temperature and slight ocean wind made goose bumps appear on her legs. Since she had on Levi's shorts and a light blue blouse with a halter-top under it, the sea breeze cut right through her. Middle of the summer and the place felt cold. She couldn't imagine what the wind off that ocean felt like in the winter.

The wind whipped at her short black hair, even more so than while she was driving with the top down.

Note to self: Don't come back to the Oregon Coast in the winter.

Along the two-lane coast highway small wooden buildings seemed to huddle together, forming a sort of downtown area about three blocks long. A couple antique stores, an old-style theater, and a small grocery store that she could see. The ocean roared down the hill to one side, steep mountains climbed away from the town on the other side. It felt like the town was just hanging onto the side of the

hill, hoping to not get blown away in a big storm.

She took a deep breath, letting the thick ocean air clear her mind as she moved her shoulders and arms around to loosen up tight muscles. There was a slight hint of fish in the air, and ocean salt. She could understand just from the wonderful smell why someone would live out here in the sticks, on the edge of land.

She took another deep breath of the thick air. It was almost good enough to eat.

Maybe not as good as chicken fried steak, but it could be close. Depended on how good this diner's food was.

She studied the front of the little place for a moment. It looked good, like it had top food. A person could always tell the quality of the food in a diner by how rundown a place looked. If it was rundown, but not cared for, the food sucked. But rundown and still loved, the food would be top notch.

This diner looked like it had been a shop of some sort at one point and been remodeled a few times. It now had a steep pitched roof and black shingles. The reddish/brown paint on the wood siding was peeling slightly from around the large windows across the front facing the ocean and the highway. And one roof edge was warping slightly. But the windows were clean, the sign fairly new, and no trash littered the gravel parking lot.

Rundown, but loved. She could be in for a top-notch chicken fried steak.

The door actually had a bell on it and it clanged softly as she entered. Oh, how perfect!

Then things just got better. The freshly baked bread smell hit her like a hammer and she just stopped with sensory overload. Ocean breezes outside and fresh bread inside. Clinging to the side of a hill trying not to slip into the ocean might be worth it just for the smells.

Four empty booths filled the area under the front windows, another on the end next to what looked like a real Wurlitzer Bubbler jukebox. That thing had to be worth thousands. It wasn't on at the moment and instead some oldies radio station played faintly in the background, not loud enough to be distracting.

A Formica-topped counter ran along the back wall with eight bar stools attached to the floor in front of it with cracked red leather seats. She was in diner cliché.

Or maybe she was still back in her hotel room a hundred miles back down the beach dreaming of this place.

She was the only customer, so she had her choice of where to sit, so she headed for the counter and grabbed the stool third from the end on the left, facing the kitchen window where the sounds of pots banging could be heard. The cash register, an old black one with real push keys, covered the far left end of the counter.

The leather seat felt cold against the back of her legs, but not sticky. Another good sign.

"Hi," a woman said to Kelli, smiling as she came out of the kitchen area in the back wiping her hands on a white towel. "Howya doin'?"

The women was taller than Kelli's five-six by a good six inches and had wide, square shoulders and a face that looked square as well. A big woman with

Former PGA Golf Professional and USA Today *bestselling writer Dean Wesley Smith walks you step-by-step, club-by-club from your car to the first tee and beyond in a laugh-out-loud style that not only teaches, but entertains.*

A perfect gift for the golfer in your family.

Now Available
from all your favorite booksellers in trade paper and electronic editions.

dark hair pulled back and a wide smile that filled her almost oversized face. Her accent told Kelli she was from the Chicago area of the Midwest.

"Doing great," Kelli said. "Hungry. How's your chicken fried steak?"

"Best on da coast," the women said. "Comes with potatoes, yellow corn, and a fresh dinner roll. Choice of clam chowder or a salad to start. Eight-ninety-nine."

"The rolls are what I'm smelling?" Kelli asked.

"Sure are," the women said. "Dave just took them out of the oven, so they'll be really hot and soft."

"Perfect," Kelli said. "Chowder to start, with a cup of coffee."

Her mouth was already watering and her stomach growling as the women turned and went back into the kitchen without writing any kind of ticket up. She had only had a sandwich for lunch about three hours before, so this was perfect.

Behind her the door chimed and she glanced around to see a state cop come in. He was a looker, with deep blue eyes and a handsome square face. He had on a leather jacket and all the stuff police lugged around with them on his belt. He smiled at her and she smiled back as he took a seat in one of the booths looking out the window.

This little town was really starting to look up. A great diner and a handsome man, all in the same five minutes. She was a writer, she didn't need to live anywhere. She might think of staying here for a short time, although if she did that she would miss her office in her home in Las Vegas. She loved that book-filled, light-filled room. She had already been away from it almost too long.

Of course, the ghost was still fifteen minutes from walking through the door and changing everything.

CHAPTER TWO

July 14th, 2016
Oregon Coast

THE WILD PACIFIC OCEAN pounded on black rocks to Jesse Parks' left as the coast highway wound around a sharp ridge in a mountain and went into a massive tunnel through tall pine trees that made the bright sunny day seem suddenly dim. He loved the beauty and extreme ruggedness of the Oregon Coast. Not as much as he loved his home in the remote Valley County in Idaho, just miles from the small tourist town of McCall. But the coast was a close second in his heart.

Jesse Parks glanced at the tablet-sized tracker sitting on the passenger seat of his Jeep SUV and made note that Kelli Rae had stopped about ten minutes ahead. More than likely to get something to eat in the small town of Whale Port.

He had been following her for two days now as she made her way slowly up the Oregon Coast. She clearly hadn't been in a hurry to get anywhere and so far today had only covered about a hundred miles in just about six hours. She seemed to stop for anything that looked interesting.

For a week before that he had learned more about her than he wanted to admit. But to learn about a target was his job, what Duster Kendal had hired him to do for some reason.

He hadn't let her see him in all the time he had been following her and researching her, but now seemed like as good a time as any to get a little closer. In another day or so he was going to report back to Duster his findings and get home to Valley County.

There was nothing at all unusual about Kelli Rae that he could find. She worked too hard, did more research than anyone ever needed to do, and seemed to enjoy her life from moment to moment. She had two doctorate degrees in various aspects of historical research and a number of masters' degrees along the same lines, including one in library science.

She was as Duster had hoped she might be. A really, really good historian. Why Duster was interested was beyond Jesse, but he made it a practice to not ask clients why there were interested in researching someone. Just better that way.

He was really starting to miss his big log home and all the openness of the land and mountains around it. Even though the Oregon Coast was beautiful and rugged, he was going to need to get back to the real mountains.

Kelli Rae was a bestselling writer of true historical crime books, with the multiple degrees in history and criminology to back her up. Her books and research all focused on crimes that had occurred in the past in the western part of the United States. A strange thing to focus on and write about, but it had made her millions, and from what Jesse could tell, her research was unimpeachable. At least that's what all the critics said. Considering how much time she spent at it, there was no wonder.

He had no idea what she was researching on this trip. He hadn't gotten into her notes to find that out. He had snooping limits.

She was twenty-eight, lived alone in Las Vegas and had no family. She didn't drink or gamble that he could tell, and she also had more money than Jesse bet she even realized, considering how little she paid attention to her own finances.

Finances he had snooped into. And sadly, as most people, she had made his job very easy on that regard. But from what he could tell, no one was taking any money from her. She seemed to have an honest accountant.

She was twenty-eight and had no love interest of any type past a few brief one-night-stands. Considering how much her research and writing seemed to eat up all her time, that didn't surprise Jesse in the slightest. The woman was flat driven.

Not at all like Jesse, who had the attitude of his favorite character, Travis McGee written by a writer by the name of John D. McDonald. Jesse worked when he wanted to or when something interested him or when a favorite client asked for a favor. Duster and his wife, Bonnie, were his friends, and paid him far, far too much when he had worked for them before.

This time they had asked him to help on looking into Kelli Rae's past. He had said yes without even asking why. For Bonnie and Duster, he would do damn near anything.

In fact, about five years before, Duster had suggested that Jesse get a long oil-cloth duster like Duster wore no matter the heat or the cold. Jesse was doubtful at first, but after a few times wearing the long and very light coat, Jesse couldn't imagine being without it.

He had gone out and bought four light brown dusters and wore a light brown cowboy hat as well. Duster wore darker coats and hats. But since Jesse was almost as tall as Duster at six-one, they looked like a formidable pair when together. Like two sheriffs right out of the Old West.

Early on, right out of college, Jesse had built a reputation of being the best private investigator in the west. He had helped keep a very rich man out of jail on a crime he didn't commit, and on another he had found an online stalker's real home address for a rich client to get that stopped.

Those two things, along with hiring a great computer crew for his office in McCall to do basic background searches on new hires for about a hundred different companies and organizations from around the west, had made his name.

And his fortune.

And every so often he worked for Duster researching other historians and mathematicians. He had no idea why. He just did what Duster asked.

The small town of Whale Port, Oregon, appeared as he came around a sharp corner in the highway. The town consisted of maybe fifty buildings, at most, on a ledge between high tree-lined mountains above it and sharp rocks and pounding surf below it. The town existed at all because just on the other side of town was a small bay and river coming into the ocean. Jesse knew it was deep enough for some fishing boat docks.

Most of the fishing was gone now, but the town hung on with a two story white historical hotel, a few bed and breakfast buildings, a general store, some antique stores, a small grocery store, and two restaurants. All looked like they could use a good coat of paint, but considering the weather here, more than likely they had all been painted just last summer.

Kelli Rae's blue BMW sat in front of one of the restaurants that looked like an old diner and was clearly well kept up.

At least she had good choices in places to eat. So far, in all his research, Jesse had found very few things he didn't like about the woman, including her looks. If he didn't have such a solid rule about getting involved with a target, he would have been interested.

He pulled in and parked between her car and a State Police car. Time to get a little closer to his target before heading home to Idaho. And besides, he was hungry.

He slipped on his cowboy hat and then slipped into his duster as he climbed out. Might as well not try to hide at all. She would remember him from this point forward.

And he liked the idea of that for some reason.

CHAPTER THREE

July 14th, 2016
Oregon Coast

KELLI HAD JUST finished her clam chowder when the door chime rang behind her. The chowder was just about as good and rich and thick as she could ever remember having. Melted butter floating on the top and the spoon just stuck straight up in the chowder when served. If she hadn't seen it and tasted it, no amount of convincing would have told her chowder could be that good, that thick, that melt-in-the-mouth rich.

She pushed the cup that was closer to the size of a bowl forward, wiped her mouth, and glanced around at the new arrival in the diner.

The man looked like he had stepped out of a western novel. He wore a long tan oilcloth duster, a matching cowboy hat, and jeans and cowboy boots.

He took off his hat and then slipped out of his coat. He moved like a well-oiled machine, with no extra movement at all. He hung both the coat and the hat up on a coat tree near the right end of the counter.

He had shoulders that seemed to be solid muscle and his hips and legs were long and thin. Wow, two stunning men in the same diner at the same time. On the Oregon Coast in the middle of nowhere.

She was really, really going to need to think about staying here a little while. Maybe grab a night in the old hotel if she could get one of these men to buy her a late drink after dinner.

She must be getting horny, since she clearly hadn't had thoughts like this for some time. Too much time on this research trip, more than likely.

Then the new arrival hunk-of-a-man turned and sat down on the second counter stool from the right.

Two seats from her.

He glanced over at her and smiled.

And their gazes locked and she was lost in those incredible green eyes and wonderful grin.

That shocked her. He clearly was very smart. And she had an attraction to him that went a lot farther than just a one-night jump in the sack.

Wow.

He seemed shocked slightly as well as he stared at her for a few counts too long.

She didn't care. She wanted this stranger to keep right on staring. As long as she could catch her breath at some point.

She couldn't remember a man having that kind of impact on her before. Never.

Not at first glance at least.

Maybe it was the ocean air.

At that point the large woman came from out of the kitchen carrying a big plate with Kelli's chicken-fried steak, corn, and roll. It smelled wonderful and Kelli turned and smiled at the woman.

"Anythin' else?" the woman asked.

"I don't think I could eat even half of this," Kelli said, laughing and shaking her head at the massive plate full of food in front of her.

"Save a little room for da pie," the woman said, smiling and moving down in front of the handsome man.

"What can I get for you, stranger?"

So the handsome man was passing through as she was. Interesting.

"I'll have what she's having," he said, his voice deep and sexy. "That looks amazing?"

"I'll let you know in just one bite," Kelli said.

Then as the woman and the handsome man watched, she cut a piece of the chicken fried streak that seemed far more tender than it should be, then making sure it had some white gravy on it, she put it in her mouth.

Warm temperature, pepper taste to the gravy, and an explosion of tastes as she bit into the meat. How was this possible? The best clam chowder and now the best chicken fried steak. She had found heaven.

It might take her a couple days on the treadmill at home to work this meal off, but she didn't care. It was worth it.

She gave a two-thumbs-up sign and both the handsome man and the woman behind the counter laughed.

Damn, Kelli liked his laugh as well.

"Drink?" the woman asked.

"Coffee," the man said. "Black, and a cup of the chowder."

Kelli ate while the handsome man checked his phone for messages, then put it away as the clam chowder was brought to him.

"The spoon is sticking up in the chowder," the handsome man said, sounding stunned, "and the chowder is cover in melted butter."

"It gets even better when you taste it," Kelli said, glancing at him.

And it was right at that moment, right as she was about to take another bite of the chicken fried steak, she knew she was looking at a ghost.

Holy crap, how was that possible?

She never forgot a face and a name, especially a handsome one. It was one of her many talents that helped her in her research.

She glanced at the duster and hat hanging on the coat tree as the handsome ghost worked at the chowder.

"Excuse me," she said, trying her best to smile at him. "Can I ask you your name?"

He nodded, wiped the chowder off his lips, and extended his hand. "My name is Jesse Parks."

She shook his hand, could feel the attraction, everything, except she knew somehow she was either looking at a ghost, or a man who had lived a very, very long time.

Or she had just uncovered an amazing fraud.

"Kelli Rae," she said.

"The writer?" he asked.

She nodded and let go of his hand, even though she didn't want to. She wouldn't have minded holding that hand and other parts of him for some time.

Then she slid off her stool and pointed to the steak. "Don't let her take that. I'm far from done. I just need to get my laptop."

Jesse Parks looked puzzled, his green eyes suddenly filled with worry.

She laughed. "Don't worry. I just have to show you something. You remind me of someone is all."

With that she went out the door and to her car and quickly fished out her laptop.

There had to be a logical explanation for what was happening. He wasn't really a ghost or a very long-lived man. She knew that wasn't possible. Maybe he had a family member or something along those lines.

But this was really the strangest thing she could have ever imagined. She just hoped this didn't get in the way of jumping that handsome man's body in a hotel room somewhere around here.

CHAPTER FOUR

July 14th, 2016
Oregon Coast

JESSE INSTANTLY WORRIED he had done something wrong as Kelli, in her short jean cut-offs and light shirt, went out the door. The state cop sitting in the booth working on a sandwich watched her out the window, just in case she was some sort of nut case who was running on her meal tab.

Jesse knew that wasn't the case, since he knew how rich Kelli really was. And taking anything was not in her make-up at all. She investigated historical crimes, not committed any.

The woman came out of the kitchen and glanced at the back toward the restrooms.

"She went to get her laptop," Jesse said. "Warned me to not let you touch that, but it looks so good I'm tempted to sneak a bite."

The woman laughed. "Ya got your own coming."

At that moment Kelli came back through the door carrying a laptop computer without a case or anything. Jesse knew she had a black case for that, but more than likely had just left it in her car.

She put the black computer down on the counter between them, opened it up and while it powered up, she took another bite of chicken fried steak.

After a moment she expertly opened up a file and looked at it, shaking her head.

Then she looked up at him. "You said you name was Jesse Parks?"

Jesse nodded. What had she discovered about him.

"You have family that were here in the Pacific Northwest back around 1908? A great-grandfather or something?"

He shook his head. "All my family are from the east and Canada. I'm the first one out here. I live in central Idaho."

"How central?" she asked, looking up. Her dark eyes were intense and focused.

"Valley County," he said. "Near McCall."

"I got this picture from the Idaho Historical Society," she said, indicating a picture on her computer. "I confirmed it to be authentic and from the archives of the photographer who was working in central Idaho mining towns around the turn of the last century."

"Okay," he said, feeling very puzzled.

"I have a perfect memory for faces and names," she said. "That's why you startled me when you introduced yourself."

She swung the laptop around so he could see it and slid it toward him, then went back to her steak.

The picture was captioned "1908 Roosevelt, Idaho." It showed three men in conversation and a woman with her back turned slightly to the camera looking at something behind the group.

The photo was black and white and actually fairly clear. The three men were standing on a plank sidewalk and the main street of Roosevelt stretched beyond them.

Roosevelt looked like most mining towns of that time, with some single-story buildings next to two-story buildings. There were signs on the buildings, but he couldn't read any of them because of the angle of the photo.

Clearly the men did not know they were being photographed since the woman was slightly blurry as were the hands of two of the men.

Jesse was standing on the left of the picture, wearing his duster and cowboy hat.

Along the bottom of the photo his name was printed there.

And even more shocking was that beside him were Duster Kendal and Madison Rogers, with their names printed on the bottom of the picture as well. Duster was wearing his long coat and dark cowboy hat. Madison was wearing period clothing.

Jesse knew Madison because Jesse had done the same kind of research he was doing on Kelli on Madison a few years before.

Then Jesse looked down the counter at Kelli, at her short black hair, her size, and so on, and then back at the woman in the picture. In the weeks he had been studying Kelli Rae, he had seen photos of her from a hundred different angles.

The woman with her back slightly to the camera was Kelli, dressed in riding clothes of the period. Of that he had no doubt.

What the hell was going on?

The picture had to be a fake, but how or why?

And who would do something like this?

CHAPTER FIVE

July 14th, 2016
Oregon Coast

KELLI WORKED AT the fantastic chicken fried steak, but her attention wasn't on the steak as much as she would have liked. It was on Jesse Parks' reaction to the photo.

At first he looked puzzled, then his handsome face turned white.

Completely white as he stared at the photo. Shocked white was not a good color on his rugged, handsome face.

Then, as she was taking another bite, he had glanced at her, then back at the photo.

"This has to be a fake," Jesse said, pushing the laptop back to her as his plate full of chicken fried steak arrived.

"Besides the fact that you couldn't be in 1908, why do you think that?" Kelli asked, smiling and glancing at the picture.

"Take a close look at the woman in the picture," he said. "That's you."

Kelli started to open her mouth, then actually looked at the woman half turned in the photo and knew instantly he was right. It was her in period clothes.

"I know your books," Jesse said. "Enjoyed them, actually. Someone must be pulling a publicity gag on you. Or trying to discredit your research in some way."

"Wow," Kelli said, staring at the photo. "That is some fine work because I have fifty other pictures of the man beside you in this photo from other times and places throughout the west. That's part of what made me think this was legit. And the style of the photographer who took it as well."

She started to close her laptop, shaking her head that she had made such a boneheaded research mistake when Jesse said, "Hold on, what do you mean you have other images of the other man?"

"A lot," she said. "He pops up from about 1880 to 1930 as a marshal in many western towns. He was a real person and his identity is authenticated in numbers of ways. He never got any publicity and has never been investigated. But he was an interesting man, of that there was no doubt."

Again the handsome Jesse Parks' face had gone almost as white as the gravy on the chicken fried steak and he sat there, shaking his head. "Marshal Duster Kendal?" he asked.

She nodded.

"How many pictures would you say you have of him?" Jesse asked after a moment.

"Over fifty at least," she said, frowning. "Maybe more. From a couple dozen different photographers and sources from all over the west. Duster Kendal was a major figure in the Old West. Why?"

Jesse just sat there, staring at his food.

"Give me a minute to try to explain," he said. "Although I have no explanation for that picture. None."

Then he dug into his chicken fried steak and the color came back to his face.

She went back to eating and they sat there in silence, not at all the way she had hoped this would end up.

Now Available
from all your favorite booksellers in trade paper and electronic editions.

DEAN WESLEY
SMITH
USA Today BESTSELLING AUTHOR

AVALANCHE
CREEK
A THUNDER MOUNTAIN NOVEL

CHAPTER SIX

July 14th, 2016
Oregon Coast

JESSE HAD NO idea what to do. None of this could be real, of course, but who could be playing that kind of scam on Kelli? And such an extensive scam.

And including him and Duster and Madison in the picture? He had heard Bonnie call Duster "Marshal" numbers of times when they were together.

But Duster had never met Kelli. Jesse knew that. And Jesse had only met Madison once since he had done all the investigating on him.

So this just flat made no sense in any way.

No one could tie the four people in that picture together in any way.

He took another bite of the wonderful steak, then got off the stool.

"Don't let her take that," he said to Kelli, pointing to his half-finished plate.

"I think I heard that somewhere before," she said, smiling.

He laughed. "I'm going to make a phone call that might get us both an explanation of that picture."

Kelli looked stunned. "How could you do that? Who are you?"

Damn, he was going to have to explain himself, tell her what he had really been doing. He had never had this happen in all his years of being an investigator.

"I'll explain when I get back in a second," Jesse said and strode out the door without his hat and coat, the phone in his hand already dialing Duster's number.

He stood by his Jeep, looking out over the rough ocean, trying to calm himself. The cool ocean breeze helped a lot to clear his mind.

After a moment, Duster answered.

"Jesse," Duster said. "How's it going with Kelli Rae?"

"Up until a few moments ago," Jesse said, "just perfectly. She's as clean as they come and as dedicated a historical researcher as I have ever seen."

"Great," Duster said. "Thought so. So what happened?"

"We're on the Oregon Coast," Jesse said. "I have no idea what's she's researching, but she's been on the coast for a few days. I went into the same restaurant she was having dinner in a few minutes ago and she instantly recognized me."

"Slipping up there, old friend?" Duster asked, laughing.

"No," Jesse said. "She recognized me from a photo she had. The photo is of you and me and Madison standing on a sidewalk in Roosevelt, Idaho, in 1908. She was also in the photo, but she didn't recognize herself until I pointed it out."

Silence.

Duster Kendal said nothing.

"You still there?" Jesse asked.

"I am," Duster said.

"So who could pull this kind of scam on her," Jesse asked, "with all of us included and why? Anyone but you and Bonnie know I've been investigating her?"

"No," Duster said.

"Got any idea what is going on?" Jesse asked. "How Madison got into a picture like that?"

"I do," Duster said. "But I need to talk with Bonnie first. I'll call you back in ten minutes."

"It's going to be hard to hold her off that long," Jesse said.

"Take your laptop in with you," Duster said, "and set it up for a video conference call. We will want to talk with her. You have my permission to tell her what you have been doing."

"So we are going to blow my cover," Jesse said.

"Yes," Duster said. "But your job is clearly far from done."

With that Duster hung up.

Jesse now was more confused than he had been when he came out of the diner. He grabbed his laptop from the back seat of his Jeep and went back into the wonderful-smelling diner.

Kelli Rae glanced back at him and smiled. "Mystery solved?"

"I think I just made it worse," Jesse said, getting back on his stool and putting his laptop beside hers on the counter.

"Worse?" she asked, looking puzzled.

He nodded. "Yeah, a lot, lot worse. And honestly, this entire thing is making me angry. Take a look at the third man in that picture."

Kelli frowned and opened up her laptop, going easily back to the picture.

"Do you know the name under the third man?"

"Not from the past," she said. "He shows up in numbers of pictures, but usually not credited."

"Think of that name today and put the word doctor in front of it," Jesse said, taking another bite of the wonderful steak, then pulling off a piece of the soft roll. He needed the wonderful food to keep him calm here.

"Sure," Kelli said, shrugging. "There's a famous historian by the name of Madison Rogers. He writes mostly about the mine wars in Montana."

"And he's married to…?" Jesse asked.

"Historian Dawn Edwards," Kelli said, glancing at the picture again. "Her most famous book is about this town in the picture."

"I know both of them," Jesse said.

"You do?" she asked, looking up into his eyes.

"You are not going to like this part," he said.

"Fire away," she said.

"I'm a private investigator who has a firm in McCall, Idaho, and I sometimes have done background checks on mathematicians and historians for a certain client. I did one on Dawn Edwards and on Madison, the same Madison in that fake picture."

"Oh," was all Kelli said.

That was more than Jesse could think to say at the moment.

CHAPTER SEVEN

July 14th, 2016
Oregon Coast

"THIS IS JUST flat weird," Kelli said. Then what he had said suddenly dawned on her. "You are investigating me?"

Jesse pushed his plate forward and turned to face her. He was more handsome than she had realized before. And he didn't look happy. She didn't blame him and she was a long way from happy. A long damn ways. She never expected to run into a nut case tracking her out here. Especially such a good-looking one.

He nodded. "I am."

He then opened his laptop and got it going. "The couple who hired me to look into you would like to talk with you."

He pointed to the screen.

"And why would I want to talk with them?" she asked, feeling just about as angry as she had felt in a damn long time. She didn't often get really angry, but when she did, and lost control, it was never a pretty sight.

"Because that picture, when I told my client about it, rocked him. And honestly, I want to find out what the hell is exactly going on as well. That picture is not possible."

"It's a fake," she said, disgusted. "What's the big damn deal?"

"No doubt it's a fake," he said. "But how?"

"Some discrediting stunt as you said. Did you set it up?"

"You were the one that showed it to me, remember?" Jesse said. "I had no intention of doing anything but having lunch here, saying hello, and then heading back to Idaho with my job done."

"So did I come clean?" she asked, her words biting.

"I don't make judgments, I just investigate," he said. "But here is the key with that picture. Only the couple who hired me know I was doing a background check on you. For what reason, I have no idea. They did not tell me, but I would trust both of them with my life."

"So," she said, wishing the woman from the kitchen would come out of the back so she could pay and just get the hell out of here. At least the state cop was still sitting in the booth behind her if there was a problem.

"When did you get that picture?" he asked.

"About a year ago," she said, suddenly realizing how impossible that was as well.

Jesse went on. "I had never heard of your name a year ago. They did not create that picture and you didn't and I didn't create it, yet you found it a year ago and recognized me in it and showed it to me.

Something is going on we both need to know about, don't you think?"

She just shook her head. As he said, not a bit of this was making sense, and that scared her.

"As I said, I have done this for five different historians in the past for the same couple who hired me. I have also investigated an architect, an interior designer, and two mathematicians. Both the mathematicians were higher-level theorists and they both work for the couple who hired me now."

"And what do your clients do?" she asked.

"I have told you more than I should," Jesse said. "They gave me permission to blow my cover and tell you what I was doing, but beyond that let them tell you. And honestly, other than their names, I have no idea why they hired me to do a background report on you."

At that moment his computer dinged and he started up the conference call.

"Is she there?" a man's voice on the screen asked.

"She is," Jesse said. "Angry as she has a right to be, and wanting answers, as do I."

At least he acknowledged she had a right to be upset about being investigated.

"Let us talk with her," the man's voice said.

Jesse turned the computer around so that it faced Kelli.

On the screen were two people. One was a dead replica for Duster Kendal, the other a dead replica for a woman known in the San Francisco area around the turn of the century as Bonnie Kendal.

Kelli jerked back. "What the hell is going on?"

"Doctor Rae," the man said. "I would like to introduce myself. I am Duster Kendal. This is my wife, Bonnie."

"So you two have been planting the fake pictures," Kelli said.

Both of them shook their heads.

"We planted no fake pictures," Bonnie said. "And I am sorry you had to discover we were having a background check done on you before we had a chance to meet. You have a right to be angry and we apologize. We have an offer for you and it is sensitive and we needed to know who you really are before making the offer. Nothing more than that."

Kelli shook her head. "I have no idea who you are, I don't need a job, and I sure don't need some private detective following me around."

She glanced at Jesse when she said that, but he was looking down at his almost empty coffee cup just shaking his head.

"We don't expect you to trust us," Duster said. "And we were never going to offer you a job. We were going to offer you a way to help in your book research. Nothing more. We are sending you our history, our CVs, and so on. And we also have six others sending their backgrounds, as well as our character references to you."

"All we ask," Bonnie said, "Is that you meet us in Portland to talk with us, give us a chance to make an offer we think you might be interested in."

"Can you explain the picture?" Kelli said.

"We can, yes," Bonnie said. "We can explain them all. There is an explanation."

"I would love to hear that as well," Jesse muttered, more to himself.

Kelli sat back slightly on the stool. The idea that they weren't offering her a job and wanted to help in her research was interesting. It calmed her some.

And it calmed her that the investigator they had hired was as upset about all this

as she was. If what they had to offer was something special, of course they would have had her investigated. It was not the first time someone had looked over her life. She had nothing to hide.

So they had been following standard procedure and the picture had just knocked everything off the rails.

No one said a word as she stared at the two people facing her on the screen. They had been in so many pictures from so many collections that were authenticated, she had to know how they had done that, and why.

"Send me your information and your references," Kelli said. "Then I'll decide if I want to talk or not."

"It's in your e-mail as we speak," Bonnie said. "Have Jesse call us back after you have looked it over."

"Understood," she said.

She pushed the laptop back toward Jesse.

He turned it around. "I'm going to need an explanation for those pictures as well. And exactly why I've been doing all this. I think it's beyond time I know the reason why."

"Only fair," Kelli heard Duster say. "If Doctor Rae decides to meet us, we'll explain it to both of you in Portland. If she chooses not to, we'll show you when you get back to Boise."

"Thank you," Jesse said, closing the laptop.

She could tell he was clearly not happy either. The fake photo she had shown him had clearly stepped over some line for him as well.

And for some reason that made her feel a lot better about him.

Plus, he was just so damn good-looking. And he got even more handsome when annoyed.

CHAPTER EIGHT

July 14th, 2016
Oregon Coast

SHE CLICKED ON her e-mail and let the documents upload quickly. As they were coming up, the woman from the back room came out and cleared off their plates.

"Banana cream pie ta die for," the large woman said as she filled both their coffee cups again. "Fresh cherry pie and fresh strawberry pie as well."

"I'll take a piece of the banana cream," Jesse said.

"Same," Kelli said, "And thanks for the use of your Wi-Fi."

"Nothing like that out here on the edge of nothin'," the woman said, turning to head back into the kitchen.

Jesse pointed to his computer. "Hot spot Wi-Fi."

She nodded and said nothing, because honestly she wasn't sure what she could say at this point. So she focused on the information that had come to her computer.

It seemed Bonnie and Duster Kendal were two of the most acclaimed theoretical mathematicians working today. They both had more degrees than she did, but not in history, in high level mathematics.

She did a quick search for their records in other places. They had done some papers and from what she could tell wanted no credit for discoveries. They were acclaimed as the two most brilliant working math brains on the planet and lived a mostly secluded life in Boise.

However, they had buildings and entire wings of science and math departments named after them in numbers of universities. Clearly they had donated a ton of money.

She went to the six historians who had sent her references. Holy shit, it was the who's who of modern working historians. Five were focused in American history, one worked in World War One and pre-war Europe. All six had added notes to her simply saying in one way or another, "Trust Bonnie and Duster."

Two women who sent along letters and their backgrounds were historical designers, both working in areas of historical renovation. All of them had numbers of books out.

Clearly Bonnie and Duster had wanted to make her an offer that brought her into this group. Not at all sure why. Or what they could even offer her that she didn't already have.

She put the list of names who had sent her letters on her screen and turned it for Jesse to see. "You know these people."

He glanced at the list and nodded. "I have met them all at one point or another."

"You do background checks on all of them?" she asked.

He looked very pained at that question.

"You think Bonnie and Duster are going to care if you tell me that at this point?" she asked. She indicated the computer. "They are clearly doing their best to repair the damage from that picture at this point."

"I did," Jesse nodded, looking back at his coffee. "And they were all told I had done that after the fact, as you would have been."

"Look," she said, turning back to her computer. "I am sorry to have compromised your investigative ethics here. But to be honest with you, that picture is bothering me more than I want to think about

right now. If I can't trust what I find in major historical records, what can I trust for my books?"

He looked at her, his green eyes intense. "It's bothering me as well because a year ago no one knew I would be investigating you. Hell, I didn't even know it. That picture took time to plant. I want to know how and why someone would do that."

"So we both have the same goal here," she said. "Get some answers."

He nodded.

At that point the woman brought huge slices of pie, a couple of fresh forks, and some extra napkins. She slid the pies in front of both of them.

The slice of pie had to be a good six inches high and looked to be more like a quarter of a pie than a slice.

"Wow," Kelli said, moving her computer to the side a little. "Does this place serve anything small?"

"When ya live on the edge of da planet," the large woman said, "no point wastin' time on da small stuff."

"Amen to that," Jesse said, digging into the pie.

Kelli laughed.

And then went back to looking over the information she had been sent, looking for anything that seemed at all out of place.

CHAPTER NINE

July 14th, 2016
Oregon Coast

THEY HAD BOTH finished their huge slices of wonderful banana cream pie when Kelli finally surfaced from reading all the stuff Duster and Bonnie had sent her.

Jesse had so overstepped his bounds on this meeting, he was disgusted with himself. There were no laws governing client confidentiality with investigators, but he had his own rules. And even though Bonnie and Duster had introduced themselves, he was still angry for being put in this position.

And damn angry at whomever did that photo.

Duster had said he was done with this investigation. But it all still bothered him.

And it honestly worried him that he had made Kelli mad at him. He found her amazingly attractive and smart and more than likely funny, if the situation allowed. He hoped that they could patch this up enough to at least get to know each other a little better. Not the investigator know, but the personal knowing.

After staring off into space for a moment, she turned to him. "Your clients and their friends are some amazing people."

He nodded. "That they are, and even more amazing in real life when you meet them."

"You like them, huh?" she asked, staring into his eyes with those intense dark eyes of hers.

"More than I sometimes realize," he said. "That's why this photo stuff has me so damn bothered. It's not at all like them."

"So call them," she said. "Let's meet them in Portland and find out just what the hell this is all about."

He nodded. "I was hoping you were going to say that."

"Why?" she asked, "you get a bonus if I sign on or something?"

"I think I deserved that," he said, shaking his head and working to get his laptop going to make a connection. "I have no idea what they are going to offer you. And I sure don't need their money."

"Sorry," she said, looking worried.

"No reason to be sorry," he said. "I'd be pissed off as well in this situation. I just wanted to not have to wait until Boise to figure out what the hell is going on."

She laughed. "And I thought it was because you wanted to spend more time with my biting personality."

"Well," he said, smiling at her. "That too."

CHAPTER TEN

July 14th, 2016
Oregon Coast

KELLI WATCHED AS Jesse got the computer going, made the connection, and then said, "Hello."

"She still there or she slap you and drive off?" Duster asked, laughing.

"I've been a perfect gentleman," Jesse said, smiling. "And I wouldn't have blamed her if she did, but she's right here."

He turned the computer to Kelli, who was smiling.

"I was angry enough that I almost did just that," Kelli said. "But had to wait for my fantastic and huge piece of pie and read what you sent."

"Are you talking banana cream pie?" Bonnie asked, her eyes wide. "Are you at the Whale Port Diner?"

"We are," Kelli said, glancing at Jesse who just shrugged and mouthed the words that he didn't tell them.

"Say hi to Betsy for me," Bonnie said.

"And I hope like hell you had the chicken fried steak," Duster said.

"We both did," Kelli said. "It was heavenly."

"Always is," Duster said.

At that moment, the large woman from the back came out. "Did I hear my name?"

Kelli swung the computer around and the large woman lit up. "Bonnie! Duster! When the hell are you two going ta drag your sorry asses back out here for a dinner and some cards?"

Kelli heard both Bonnie and Duster laugh. "We've been hoping to do just that very soon."

"Got your favorite stools ready for ya," she said. "These two computer geeks sitting at my counter with ya?"

"They are," Duster said. "Or at least one of them is and the other we hope to meet with soon."

"Figures," the large woman said, smiling. "You two always attract the brainy kind. See ya soon."

"Bye, Betsy," both Bonnie and Duster said as Betsy turned the computer around.

Both Bonnie and Duster were smiling like she had just given them the treat of the year. Who in the hell were these two mathematicians, anyway?

"I'll meet with you in Portland," Kelli said.

Both Bonnie and Duster kept smiling, but there was a serious note behind the smile suddenly.

"It will take you about three hours to drive and get across Portland to the airport," Duster said. "There's a good restaurant near the airport on Airport Way called Bill's Steakhouse. How about we meet you there in three hours. I'll have a back room reserved so we can talk in private."

"That sounds fine with me," Kelli said.

She glanced at Jesse who just shrugged and nodded.

"We'll both be there," Kelli said.

"Call if either of you have traffic problems."

And then the screen went dark.

She pushed the computer back to Jesse who shut it.

"They have their own jet, huh?" she said.

"I honestly didn't realize that until right now," he said.

At that moment Betsy came out from the kitchen again. "Dinner is on us."

"No need to do that," Jesse said a moment before Kelli could.

"See that new grill back there," she said, pointing back into the kitchen. "And when ya go outside, notice the new roof on da place. All Bonnie and Duster. And they fixed up our home too and funded us enough capital to keep goin' without worry. Only deal was that we keep on doin' what we were doin' and serving great food."

"You have any idea why?" Kelli asked.

Betsy shook her head. "This place had been in operation for goin' on one hundred and twenty years and without them, it would be shut down. They wanted nothing in return. No other strings, no loan, nothin'. Amazin' people. And they did the same thing for da historic hotel down the street. Helped them remodel and get back on their feet and stay open as well. It started just ahead of this place opening. And they would never tell us why."

With that, Betsy turned away, smiling.

Kelli glanced over at Jesse, who was shaking his head and watching Betsy walk away.

"Didn't know your own client that well, huh?" Kelli asked.

"Clearly not," Jesse said. "And in about three hours I want to start remedying that situation."

"Yeah," Kelli said. "Some answers would sure be nice."

With that they both left a twenty-dollar tip near their pie plates, and with laptops in hand, headed for their cars.

Outside, in the fresh ocean air, Kelli glanced over the top of her car at the handsome face of Jesse. "Since you've been following me for some time now, how about I follow you to Portland?"

"Seems more than fair enough," he said, smiling at her.

And that smile she could get used to, if first she got some answers.

PART TWO
An Offer

CHAPTER ELEVEN

July 14th, 2016
Portland, Oregon

JESSIE WAS IMPRESSED that Kelli stayed right behind him all the way from Whale Cove into the west side of Portland and then through Portland to the airport on the east side.

They made the drive in just under three hours.

He would have been much happier if they had been riding together, but after a while he was glad they weren't. The drive gave him time to think and calm down.

And more than likely it gave Kelli the same thing. Bonnie and Duster had always been full of surprises for him, and clearly others around them as well. Now he needed to know why they had had him investigating all these people over the years.

And how that picture of him standing in Roosevelt, Idaho, in 1908 could even have been done. Especially a year ago, as Kelli claimed it was.

Because that wasn't possible.

What he hadn't told Kelli was that the metal bracelet on his wrist, the one that could be seen in the picture, he hadn't got as a gift until last Christmas. A year ago he didn't have that metal on his wrist.

So either she was lying about when she got the picture, or something else really ugly was going on.

Kelli pulled up and parked beside him in the large, paved parking lot of Bill's Steakhouse. The heat of the July evening in Portland was a strong contrast to the cool ocean breeze on the coast. He could hear the roar of a jet taking off over the traffic sounds of the nearby five-lane road.

The wonderful smell of steaks being grilled filled the air around them. The steakhouse was dark wood with a ton of plants around it, almost hiding it from the parking lot and road. It had a dark, low-pitched roof and dark-tinted windows.

Since it was almost nine in the evening, the sun was starting down over the west hills and there were only about ten other cars in the parking lot.

Kelli got out, a notebook in hand, and smiled at him as she headed for the front door of the restaurant. "Sorry to be in a rush, but that coffee on the coast has been demanding an exit for the last hour."

"Yeah," he said, following her. "Thought about stopping and then just got thinking."

He got to the door ahead of her and held it open.

"Thinking about me, I hope," she said, brushing past him, smiling, then turning and heading for the restroom sign.

"Who else," he said, laughing and following her.

"Right answer," she said as she pushed open the women's room door and went in.

After clearing out the coffee from the previous meal, he headed back into the dark, wood and plant restaurant. Everything was made of dark wood planks and the floors were stained a lighter oak color. Plants of all sizes and forms seemed to be filling every nook and cranny in the place. All the sounds in the place felt muffled from all the plants.

The place smelled of steak, almost so thick it was amazing the walls and the leaves weren't coated in steak grease.

He went back to the wooden front desk where a young college-aged girl with pixie brown hair greeted him with a bright smile.

"Duster Kendal party?" Jesse asked. "Are they here?"

"They are," the young hostess girl said. "Follow the main aisle all the way to the back. Door labeled Stetson."

"Find them?" Kelli asked, coming up to him as he was about to head for the back.

"They are here," Jesse said, nodding. "Follow me."

"Twice in one day," she said, laughing.

Clearly she was in a much better mood after calming down and the drive.

When they had wound their way to the Stetson room in the back, Jesse opened it for her and she went into the small banquet room ahead of him. It also looked like the rest of the restaurant, with wood planks on the walls and plants hanging from high rafters, as well as sitting in corners.

A table for six was set. Duster and Bonnie sat at one end, with Duster at the head of the table. Dawn Edwards and Madison Rogers sat in the middle on one side.

All of them stood as they came in.

Bonnie was dressed in her casual look. Dark slacks, a light-blue silk blouse, and she had her long brown hair pulled back. Bonnie was tall, just a few inches shorter than he was. She had a classic beauty that was hard to ignore.

Duster had his long coat hanging up on a coat rack to the right of the table near a tall tree-like plant and his cowboy hat on the stand as well. He wore his brown hair cut short and had on a simple blue dress shirt with the sleeves rolled up. He was as tall as Jesse, but seemed to command a room more than any person Jesse had ever met.

Madison was about Bonnie's height at around five-foot-nine, had dark hair, and also was dressed casually in dark slacks and a dark blue shirt with the sleeves buttoned.

Dawn was the shortest one of the group by a long ways, but looked thin and strong. She had long brown hair, also pulled back, and wore the same casual style as the rest with dark jeans and a silk blouse with no jewelry.

"Glad you made the drive from the coast safely," Bonnie said, coming forward first to shake Kelli's hand. Then Duster shook her hand, then Bonnie turned and introduced her to Dawn and Madison.

From what Jesse could tell, Kelli was stunned to meet them here.

"Honored," she said to both of them. "I am such a fan of your books."

"And we are of yours as well," Dawn said.

Jesse shook all their hands as well, even though he knew them all. He had investigated both Dawn and Madison at one point. But he hadn't seen them for almost a year.

Then Jesse went to a spot beside Bonnie so that Kelli could have the place at the end of the table, facing Duster.

As they all got seated, Madison said to her. "I hear you discovered you were being vetted before you should have discovered it?"

Kelli laughed. "Yeah, an accident. I just never forget a face and I had seen Jesse's face in a picture from Roosevelt Idaho in 1908 and knew that couldn't be. At first I thought he was a ghost or something."

"He is such a good investigator," Duster said, smiling, "I've often wondered if he was a ghost."

"So how could he be in that picture?" Kelli asked, getting right to the point.

Jesse watched as Bonnie and Duster and Dawn and Madison all had to suddenly look down at their plates or straighten their napkins or something.

Kellie glanced at Jesse with a puzzled look and he just shrugged. He had no idea what was going on. Not a clue.

After a moment a waiter wearing western jeans and a cowboy red and black plaid shirt came out of the back with menus and some drinks for the four of them, then he took Kelli and Jesse's drink order and left. Both of them once again ordered coffee.

"Before we try to even begin to explain all this," Bonnie said, "can I ask what you were doing at our favorite all time historical diner on the coast?"

"Been following a trail for my research," Kelli said. "The diner was just a lucky find."

Madison and Dawn looked at Kelli and then at Jesse. "Don't tell me you guys had dinner at the Whale Cove Diner?"

Jesse laughed. "We did, and yes, we had the chicken fried steak and banana cream pie."

Madison turned to Duster. "What the hell are we doing here? We should be over there eating."

Both Bonnie and Duster laughed. "We figured that if we gave Doctor Rae here too much time to think about all this, she would bolt."

"Call me Kelli," she said. "And you might have been right."

"So can I ask what you were researching?" Dawn asked. "Another past crime I hope?"

Kelli glanced at Jesse. "You know, don't you?"

He just shook his head. "I just vet a person's past stuff, criminal actions, that sort of thing. I don't snoop into e-mails or private research or anything like that."

"Oh, sorry," she said, looking at him with a worried expression.

He nodded back at her that it was all right. Again he didn't blame her at all.

She turned to Dawn. "I've been following the possible theft of about 30 Season Medals that Lewis and Clark gave out to Native American leaders during their trip."

Jesse had no idea what she was talking about, but clearly Dawn and Madison did.

"Season Medals?" Dawn asked. "I thought Lewis and Clark gave away all fifty-five of them that they had on that first expedition."

"They did," Jesse said. "But starting around 1880 or so, a man by the name of John Simon Bushnell started a quest to buy or barter from the Native Americans as many of the medals as he could get back."

"He did?" Madison asked. "Wow."

Kelli nodded. "He is rumored to have managed to get thirty or more of the Season Medals by 1906. He was shot in Roosevelt, Idaho, at some point, no one is certain by who or why. His name is on the plaque there in the Roosevelt cemetery."

Jesse was fascinated. He liked her books and this sounded like she could make this story riveting.

"And the medals vanished with his death?" Duster asked.

"They did," Kelli said, nodding. "But since he was shot, there is speculation that the medals were stolen from him. He had been along the Oregon Coast before going to Roosevelt, so I was tracking any evidence I could find along the coast before heading to Roosevelt."

"Do you remember the man's name she is tracking?" Duster asked Dawn and Madison.

"No," they both said at the same time.

"But I do remember," Dawn said, "that someone was shot in a small cabin near Roosevelt in late October one year, after the valley had already closed up for the winter because of snow. It never crossed my research as important, so I paid it no attention."

"So these medals would be worth something if found today?" Jesse asked.

"Besides historical importance," Kelli said, "a great deal of money. A few that have surfaced that are authenticated that Lewis and Clark gave away have sold at upwards of hundreds of thousands each."

"A million dollar lost treasure," Jesse said, nodding.

"A fascinating crime in my opinion," Kelli said. "Great history that most don't know about wrapped into a crime. A perfect book."

The other four at the table nodded.

Jesse couldn't agree more.

At that point the waiter came back with his and Kelli's drinks, then took all their orders and left.

"Since you won't explain the picture, what's this offer?" Kellie asked Bonnie and Duster as the waiter left.

Jesse loved how Kelli just dove right at the point.

But again, just silence filled the room.

CHAPTER TWELVE

July 14th, 2016
Portland, Oregon

KELLI STARED AT the silent four, then said, "Let me make this simple for you. First tell me how I found a picture of three of you and me standing on a wooden sidewalk in Roosevelt, Idaho?"

Duster laughed. "That's like the hardest question you could ask."

Kelli noted that Dawn and Madison both nodded.

"Let me start a little before that," Bonnie said. "I will tell you that the photo is accurate, taken by the photographer who is credited for the picture. I know that without looking at it because none of us here have any reason to doctor any pictures for any reason."

Duster and Dawn and Madison all nodded.

"You said you got that picture from the Idaho historical society about a year ago. Right?" Jesse asked her.

Kelli nodded, not having any clue as how to make sense of what Bonnie said.

"And that picture is a digital copy or a paper copy?"

"Both," Kelli said, looking at Jesse. "On the paper copy I have the copyright information on the back, when I obtained it, and so on. Then I scanned all pictures in to take with me for reference if needed."

Jesse pointed to a wide silver metal bracelet on his wrist. "I have been wearing this since I bought it from an artist outside of Cascade, Idaho, just six months ago."

Kelli nodded.

"I am wearing it in the photo," Jesse said.

Kelli could feel a cloud of confusion crossing over her mind. How in the hell could that be possible?

Then Jesse turned to the rest of the table. "I know, for some reason, you want Doctor Rae here to understand, to help her with her research. But I've been friends with you all for years. I think as a friend I'm owed a clear explanation. Don't you?"

All four nodded.

"We did not doctor any photos," Bonnie said. "That photo, if it says it was taken in 1908, and you have it authenticated, was taken in 1908 in Roosevelt, Idaho."

"Now you're starting to make me mad," Jesse said, sitting back.

Duster looked at Kelli. "Doctor Rae, you read the information we sent you? Jesse knows us all, but you need to be up to speed with who we are."

"I read it," Kelli said. "And did a little more digging on my own." She kept her voice low and even because she was getting just as angry as Jesse.

"We are both theoretical mathematicians," Duster said indicating himself and Bonnie. "We specialize in the theory of alternate timelines. And how matter and energy and time are all wrapped in together."

Kelli nodded for Duster to go on.

"In our theories, we suggest, and have proven, that there is a physical hub where all alternate universes express themselves in a physical form."

"You are losing me quickly," Kelli said.

"Think of it this way," Bonnie said. "If Jesse had decided to just wait in his car for you to finish dinner in Whale Cove instead of going inside, and you would have never seen him, we all would not be sitting here right now. That's an alternate universe from the one we are in."

"Every decision we make, big or small, creates another alternate universe," Duster said. "Sometimes those alternate universes just blend back into each other since the results make no long-term difference."

"So if I order steak versus a chicken here at dinner two alternate universes are created?" Kelli said. "That's silly."

"Not silly," Bonnie said. "Mathematically proven. Imagine if the chicken was tainted and you got sick because of the choice and missed an important clue in your research. But if you had the steak, you didn't get sick, wrote the book, and changed things. Every decision we make has repercussions off into the future. Most decisions change nothing, but your decision to come here when you could have just driven off is a decision."

"That's billions of timelines," Kelli said, not even able to grasp that much.

"Far, far more than that," Duster said.

"So what does all this have to do with the picture?" Jesse asked.

"You said the four of us are in the picture," Duster asked, indicating her and Jesse and Madison and himself.

Kelli nodded.

"In another alternate timeline, the four of us went back into the past, into this timeline to Roosevelt in 1908," Duster said, "more than likely to help you research your book, and without our knowing it, some photographer got our picture."

Kelli just looked at Bonnie and Duster. "You can travel back in time?"

"Back in the past of other timelines, yes," Bonnie said, "as crazy as that sounds."

"We go back to do research all the time," Dawn said. "Since almost all timelines are nearly identical to the one we are in. We have spent a lot of time in Roosevelt before the flood buried it, actually. We would love to help you research the Season Medals."

"You could even meet John Bushnell if you wanted," Madison said. "Actually find out why he was after the Season Medals in the first place."

Kelli sat back, more stunned than she wanted to admit as the waiter started to bring their food. If she wasn't sitting with two of the most respected historians in the world, and the two most acclaimed mathematicians of all time, she would be headed out the door.

And she most certainly would if she had any other explanation for that photograph.

Actually, photographs. She knew without a doubt that she was sitting across the table from one of the great Marshals of the Old West. And Bonnie Kendal was known as the Angel of San Francisco for her good deeds there.

How in the hell was this possible?

Could they really be telling the truth?

CHAPTER THIRTEEN

July 14th, 2016
Portland, Oregon

JESSE JUST SAT there staring at four people he wasn't sure he knew any more. They had just come up with the craziest story he had ever heard. And yet damned if he could think of another explanation for that photo. Or why Kelli Rae would have it.

The steak in front of him, a nice top sirloin cut, smelled wonderful. The plate had a baker on it with garnishments left on the side as he had asked. And beside his plate was a dish of steamed asparagus that looked crisp and green.

It was going on four hours since he had eaten that piece of banana cream pie, so he was hungry. He just wasn't sure, with the discussion, if he had an appetite or not.

He dug into the steak, let the wonderful, warm juicy flavor of the first bite almost melt in his mouth, and decided to just eat.

"We have no doubt," Duster said after the waiter had left, "that you both think all four of us have lost our minds."

"We both thought they were crazy," Dawn said, nodding, "the first time they told us what they were doing."

"Only way to believe it is to see the nexus," Madison said.

"The nexus?" Kelli asked, slightly before Jesse could because he was chewing on a piece of wonderful steak.

"We theorized," Bonnie said, "that all time and matter and energy come together in a physical form. We accidently found the place."

"That's the offer we wanted to make to you, Doctor Rae," Duster said. "We wanted to offer you access to the nexus for your research in your projects. No strings attached."

Kelli said nothing, looking stunned.

Jesse thought back over the people that Bonnie and Duster had had him research over the years. "How many people know about this place?"

"Fourteen," Bonnie said, "counting the six of us at this table."

"So that's why you've had me research historians and the two mathematicians that work for you," Jesse said. "But why the architect and interior designer?"

"You won't believe this anymore than anything else," Bonnie said, laughing.

"Try me," Kelli said.

"For the first number of years going back into time," Duster said, "we had always heard about a huge lodge built on Monumental Summit above the town of Roosevelt. But we could never find evidence it was there."

"Of course it's there," Jesse said. "I've even spent a few nights in it."

"As have I," Kelli said.

"That's because we went back, six of us, including the architect and a historical designer you vetted," Duster said to Jesse, "and we built the lodge."

"And at the same time," Bonnie said, "the same group of us from another timeline came to our timeline and built the lodge here."

"So the six of us all remember the lodge not being there and the lodge always being there," Madison said, shaking his head.

"It's why we hired two more mathematicians to help us figure out how that was possible," Bonnie said.

"It's the same way those pictures happened," Duster said. "It's us, but from other timelines going into the past of this timeline."

Jesse just shook his head and stared at his half-eaten steak.

Duster put down his fork and looked directly at Jesse, then at Kelli. "Here is what I would like to do, if you are

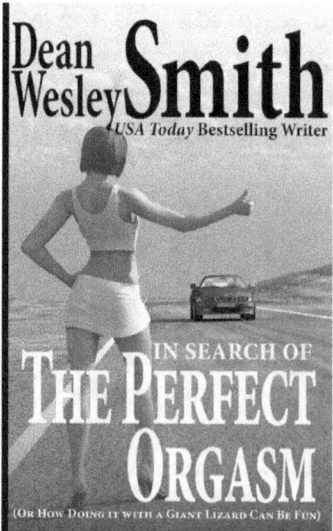

Some Classic Dean Wesley Smith Stories
Available at your favorite booksellers.

willing to trust us, give us a little rope to our crazy story, give us a chance to show you one of the great wonders of the world."

"You want to show us the nexus thingie?" Kelli asked.

"It's more like a place," Duster said, smiling. "And it's not dangerous in any fashion. Let us fly you in tomorrow morning and show you. Then, after you have seen it, you can both walk away or use it as you please for research and investigation. Our only condition is that you never tell anyone about it or write about it in any fashion."

Jesse sat back and looked at Kelli.

She seemed to be lost in thought.

Jesse knew he wanted to see it. He had been working far too long around Bonnie and Duster to not want to understand what they were really doing.

"Doctor Rae?" Bonnie asked.

"You know you are all nuts," she said.

All four of them nodded.

"If I didn't respect your work so much," she said to Dawn and Madison, "I would be long out the door."

"Can't say for an instant that we would blame you," Dawn said.

Kelli looked at Bonnie and Duster. "And I respect the work you two have done as well, even though I don't understand it. But since you are respected in your field, that helps."

Both Bonnie and Duster nodded.

"And I flat don't understand, Marshal, how you could be sitting here," Kelli said.

Jesse almost laughed as Duster jerked slightly.

"And Bonnie," Kelli said, "I know of you in history as The Angel of San Francisco. And yet here you sit as well."

"The what?" Duster asked, glancing at Bonnie.

Bonnie waved him silent.

"I have a perfect memory for faces and details," Kelli said, "and I have seen hundreds of authenticated pictures of both of you from many, many photographers. So I want to see this place as well."

Bonnie and Duster looked relieved and Dawn and Madison were smiling.

"But I have two conditions," Kelli said.

Duster and Bonnie nodded.

"First that Jesse agrees to come along."

She looked at him with those intense dark eyes.

"I wouldn't miss this for anything," Jesse said, nodding. He had no idea what he was getting himself in for, but he really wanted to keep trusting Bonnie and Duster. And it seemed that for him to do that, he was going to need to trust them just a tad bit farther.

Kelli smiled, then turned back to the other four. "My second condition is simple."

"We'll do what we can," Duster said.

"Call me Kelli," she said.

Jesse watched for a moment as the shock seemed to hit the other four, then they all laughed.

"We can do that, Kelli," Bonnie said, smiling. "We can do that."

CHAPTER FOURTEEN

July 15th, 2016
Portland, Oregon

KELLI COULDN'T BELIEVE how early Duster had wanted them up. He had gotten them all suites at a suite hotel across the parking lot from the restaurant. Kelli had kind of hoped to get to know Jesse a little better, spend some time just talking with him, but after dinner she had decided to just let that wait until they got past whatever they were going to see in the morning.

She had gone to her suite, taken a long, hot bath, and then did more research on Bonnie and Duster and Dawn and Madison.

She couldn't find a thing that made her question them in the slightest. But how could she not question such a crazy story?

Then she had looked at dozens of pictures from the past of both of them. There was no doubt it was the same two people. Sometimes they were a little older, but otherwise no difference.

She had finally drifted off after midnight.

At 5:30 a.m., Kelli found herself, with an overnight bag stuffed with some extra underwear and sleep items, standing outside of a private hanger in the Portland Airport. The rest of her stuff she had left locked in her car. The damned sun wasn't even up yet and the air had a bite to it that made her wish she had worn a light jacket. They had all been told to dress in simple hiking clothes, so she had on her jeans, a regular blouse with a sports bra under it, and her favorite tennis shoes.

The morning air was sending goose bumps up and down her arms.

They had left their cars parked in a protected area for a slight fee at the suite hotel and would come back for them in a day or so.

Duster and Bonnie were already on board the jet that sat with its lights on in front of her. It was a fairly large private jet, bigger than anything she had had the chance to fly in before. She stood on the tarmac outside the hanger, trying to get her balance. She never got up this early in the morning.

Ever.

Even a quick bite of a dried Danish and cup of horrid coffee in the hotel breakfast area hadn't even begun to dent how she felt.

"What a horrid time of the morning," Jesse said, coming out of the building behind her. He walked alongside Madison and Dawn who both carried cups of coffee.

"Duster likes to get things started early," Madison said, shaking his head.

Kelli was glad the other three looked almost as bad as she felt, even though early in the morning Jesse was still the most handsome man she had ever seen. He had on his long duster coat and cowboy hat, but he wore tennis shoes instead of cowboy boots this morning.

"We can stretch out and nap on the plane," Dawn said. "But it's a pretty short flight to Boise, so it will be a short nap."

"Anything at the moment will help," Kelli said.

All three nodded as they headed across the concrete toward the jet, carrying their day bags. Clearly Duster and Bonnie had a lot of money to afford a plane like this. Far more than she would have thought mathematicians should have.

Duster was up front talking with the pilots and Bonnie was already seated, her chair kicked back, a sleep mask on her forehead. It seemed it was too early for her as well. She had on jeans, a dark cotton blouse, and had kicked off her tennis shoes.

"Duster sits there," Bonnie said, pointing to the seat across from her. "Take any of the other seats. Sleep masks in the side pockets of each seat."

Kelli moved to one of the two seats in the back and took the one on her right. Jesse took the one on the left.

She eased the big leather chair back until it felt more like a bed than anything else and then grabbed the sleep mask.

Beside her Jesse had done the same thing after shedding his coat and hat. She was surprised that she felt so comfortable with him, was so attracted to him. It felt right for him to be beside her like this.

He glanced over and smiled at her. "Night."

With that he put on the sleep mask and crossed his hands over his chest.

She watched him for a moment, then did the same.

And the next thing she realized, he was waking her gently.

She pushed the sleep mask back, blinked at the light, and looked up into his smiling, handsome face.

"Now this is a nice way to wake up," she said. She wanted to reach up and pull his head down and just kiss him, but she didn't.

He laughed. "We've landed. Almost ready for stage two, whatever that is."

"Oh, joy," she said. "More mystery."

"Just one right after another," he said, smiling.

Damn she loved that smile.

CHAPTER FIFTEEN

July 15th, 2016
Above Silver City, Idaho

JESSE WAS SURPRISED when they left the big private jet and walked with their day bags about a hundred paces to a large, waiting helicopter. He had never had the chance to fly in a helicopter, so this would be interesting.

"Ever been in one of these?" he asked Kelli.

"Nope," she said. "A fun part of the adventure."

He made no comment to that.

Inside two pilots sat up front. They were all given helmets with microphones so they could talk with one another. He and Kelli and Dawn climbed into the third seat. He sat against the pilot's side window, Kelli tucked in beside him, and Dawn on the other side of her.

He liked being this close to Kelli. It felt right.

All three of them helped each other get buckled into the harness belts.

Duster and Bonnie and Madison got into the seat in front of them and after a moment the doors were closed.

Except for his own breathing, the helmet kept most of the sounds out.

"Where are we heading?" Kelli asked, her voice clear in his ears.

"Silver City area," Duster said.

"The ghost town?" Jesse asked.

Duster turned and indicated that no one should say a word, tapping his helmet and then indicating the pilots.

Jesse and Kelli both nodded. Clearly the pilots didn't know anything about the reason for this trip.

"We thought it would be fun to do a little exploring up in an old mining region," Bonnie said, "since all of you like history so much."

"Sounds wonderful," Dawn said, playing along.

Jesse glanced at Kelli who was smiling. Clearly she liked the game they were playing as well.

A minute later, the helicopter lifted off after getting clearance from the tower that he could hear through his helmet.

Kelli seemed startled at that, as the helicopter banked and headed to the east from the airport, gaining speed and altitude quickly.

She reached over and put her hand on his leg, as if it was a natural comforting movement.

He covered her hand and they stayed that way as the helicopter sped toward some blue mountains in the distance.

He knew those mountains as the Owyhee Mountains. They filled the southwest corner of the state and he had never had the chance to even get close to them, let alone go up to the state's most famous ghost town, Silver City.

He liked the greener area of the state in the center.

A few minutes later Duster pointed out the window. "Coming up on the Snake River."

Kelli leaned over him to see out and he leaned back a little to give her room, the pressure of her hand more on his leg.

After a moment she glanced at him.

"Fun, huh?" he asked.

She laughed and squeezed his leg. "I have a hunch the fun is only beginning."

"Sounds good to me," he said, squeezing her hand.

Then they both went back to staring out the window at the wide river below, and the mountains ahead.

After another ten minutes, the helicopter was over the tallest peaks of the mountains.

"Down in the valley below is the ghost town of Silver City," Duster said. "We just went over War Eagle Mountain."

Again Kelli leaned over him to look out, the pressure of her hand on his leg very comforting.

Another minute and the helicopter banked and headed in slowly toward a wide meadow on the top of a ridge line a ways above the old ghost town. There didn't seem to be any trees even close by and from what Jesse could tell from the intense winds from the helicopter blades, the grass was very short.

"Make sure you grab your bags," Duster said. "The pilots will not turn off the engines and will be headed back as soon as we are out."

"Keep your heads and arms down and stay low when you get out," a pilot said. "In case we're tipped slightly one way or the other. And leave the helmets on the floor in front of each seat."

After only a moment Jesse felt the helicopter touch down gently, then settle in.

"Have a nice day," one pilot said.

"We will call when we need a ride out," Duster said. "If you don't hear from us, come back at four in the afternoon."

"Understood," the pilot said.

The co-pilot was already out and he opened the large side door. Duster, Bonnie, and Madison all took off their helmets and, staying low, ran away from the helicopter along the grass-covered ridge.

Dawn went next, then Kelli took off her helmet and followed Dawn out.

He went out right behind Kelli.

The sound was intense, seeming to fill every cell of his body. The wind whipped at him and his coat as he carried his bag in one hand and his hat in the other, running bent over to where Duster and the rest stood.

As he and Kelli turned back toward the helicopter, the co-pilot was climbing back into his seat, the back door already closed.

After a moment, the co-pilot gave a thumbs-up out the window at them and the helicopter lifted off, turning after about fifty feet in the air and streaking back toward the Boise Valley in the distance.

After a moment, the intense thundering of the helicopter was replaced by almost perfect silence, broken only by a gentle morning breeze through the grass around their feet.

They were standing on what looked like a flat area of a ridge that sloped steeply off in two directions. On one side Jesse could see the Treasure Valley and Boise in the distance, and on the other side lower mountains sloping down into what looked like a flat desert.

"That beats the hell out of the road up here," Madison said.

"By about a thousand times," Dawn said.

"Just wish we could do it more," Duster said. "Just don't dare. Too many times and it would draw attention."

"The road is that bad?" Kelli asked.

"Worse than you can imagine," Dawn said, shaking her head.

Jesse had been on his share of bad mountain roads. He was glad he hadn't had to endure another one today. "So where are we, exactly."

"In the Owyhee Mountains about two thousand feet above the ghost town of Silver City, Idaho," Duster said, pointing over the ridge and down. "And our destination is about a thousand feet in that same direction."

At that Duster picked up his case and strode off along the ridge to the left on the Silver City side. With his long duster coat and cowboy hat, he looked perfectly at home.

Bonnie fell in behind him.

"Ready for the secret?" Madison asked.

Jesse glanced at Kelli who smiled and shrugged.

At this point, what choice did either of them have?

"Just one mystery right after another," he said, smiling.

CHAPTER SIXTEEN

July 15th, 2016
Above the ghost town of Silver City, Idaho

KELLI FOUND HERSELF getting winded easily after just fifteen minutes of walking, even though they were mostly walking either across the hillside, or down, on a fairly well defined trail. Finally it dawned on her why. She had spent most of the last week at sea level. Suddenly she found herself atop a fairly tall mountain.

"What's the elevation here?" Kelli asked.

"Seven thousand feet or so," Duster said over his shoulder. "We're almost there."

"Can take the breath right out of you, can't it?" Jesse said from behind her.

"That and these views can do that," she said, nodding. It really was spectacular, looking out over the distant valleys.

Finally, they came around a ridge covered with low pine trees and Duster pointed to a very steep and rough-looking trail that seemed to go almost straight down.

"That's the road in here," he said, turning and following along the hillside. She could see clear tire tracks in the ground, but she had no idea how a car could get up that steep grade, let alone not tip over along this side hill.

"See what I mean?" Dawn said from in front of Kelli.

"I don't even want to try to imagine," Kelli said.

Finally, they reached an area of trees.

"We normally park in these trees," Madison said, pointing to the trees they were walking through as Duster just kept on going toward what looked to be old mine tailings and a rough old mining shack.

The trail between the trees and the mine tailings was across what looked like a steep rockslide. It was almost straight down and Kelli could see the ghost town of Silver City below. There were about twenty buildings still standing in one form or another, and about five cars parked in front of what looked to be an old hotel.

When they all reached the flat top of the old mine tailings, Duster dropped his bag and then Bonnie did as well. The air, even though it was still fairly early in the morning, was starting to warm up, promising a very warm day ahead.

The flat-top area of the mine tailings was covered with a few dried weeds that had managed to get a hold in the rocks. Otherwise it was weather packed hard.

The old mining shack looked to be in its last moments of life. The boards were grayed out and rotted and the windows gone. The entire thing leaned sharply downhill and Kelli figured one more good winter and it would be nothing more than a pile of lumber. She had seen old buildings in ghost towns like that a lot.

Small, narrow gage mining-tracks, mostly rusted, ran from the back of the old shack and into a boarded up mine entrance that had collapsed a very long time ago. Rotted boards at one point had covered the old opening. Some good-sized small trees and brush grew out of where the mine had collapsed.

Looks like they were at their destination, but Kelli could see nothing at all that looked remotely like anything special.

She put down her night bag and moved over to the edge of the tailings. In her research, she had heard a lot about Silver City, just never had any reason to research it much for any of her books. Maybe at some point she would find a crime worth researching that brought her back here. The area had an interesting feel of desolation to it.

"Madison," Duster said, "you want to head on up the trail to see if anyone is up over the ridge there."

Madison nodded, left his bag and headed off the tailings past the cabin and up a clear trail leading up along the hillside.

He vanished for a few minutes. Then he reappeared and nodded. "Clear up that way."

Duster and Bonnie and Dawn in the meantime had taken binoculars from their packs and were slowly scouring the nearby ridges and trees.

Kelli glanced at Jesse, who was looking as puzzled as she felt. Whatever was here somewhere, Duster and the rest did not want to be seen accessing it.

"No one in sight," Duster said after a moment. "But keep an eye out for a few more minutes."

Dawn nodded and Bonnie handed Madison her binoculars as he came back to the group and Bonnie moved over to stand beside Duster.

Duster tucked the binoculars into his bag and then looked at both Jesse and Kelli. Kelli was stunned at how intense he looked right at that moment.

And Bonnie looked the same way.

"You have promised," Duster said, "to not tell anyone about any of this you are about to see."

Kelli nodded. "I respect my sources confidentiality."

"And you know me," Jesse said. "Nothing will get beyond me."

Both Duster and Bonnie nodded. Then he glanced at Madison and Dawn who were still scanning the hills around them. "Clear?"

"Clear," Madison said.

He and Dawn both went back to their bags and picked them up.

Duster took out a key from his pocket. It looked like an ancient skeleton key. He twisted the head once and suddenly Kelli got very, very worried.

Right beside the collapsed mine shaft what looked to be a very large rock slid back silently, and behind it a large metal door opened.

Dawn, Madison, and Bonnie stepped into the exposed chamber and the rock slid closed.

"Wow, that's impressive way up here," Jesse said.

"I'll explain how it's all powered later," Duster said. "Grab your stuff and lets get inside."

Kelli, still just staring at what appeared to be a massive rock, picked up her bag and stepped over next to Jesse. Duster took one more look around and then twisted the key again and the rock, silently, slid back.

"That's just stunning," Kelli said.

"That it is," Jesse said as they stepped inside with Duster and the rock slid closed, plunging them into complete blackness for a two count before a door to Kelli's right opened.

"Delay so no light escapes," Jesse said, nodding. "Nice!"

Kelli did not much like at all where she now found herself. It was clearly the old mine tunnel in the hill behind where the entrance had collapsed, with rotting old timbers and the rails for the ore car running up the middle.

Wires ran along one wall with light bulbs that let off a faintly orange glow strung every ten paces. It gave the entire thing a golden tint.

Bonnie and Madison and Dawn were nowhere to be seen, but from what she could tell, the mine turned to the right about forty paces into the hill. More than likely they were around that way.

"Nice," Jesse said, moving out into the mine tunnel and studying the beams. "All redone to be safe."

"A major earthquake wouldn't bring this tunnel down," Duster said, heading off down the tunnel.

Jesse glanced back at Kelli. "Ever been in an old mine before?" he asked.

"Not real excited about being in one now," Kelli said. And she wasn't. In fact, every voice in her body was telling her to turn and run before the old beams collapsed on all of them.

But with the rock and door now closed behind her, there was no place to run.

Jesse pointed up into the shadows above one beam. "It's been poured concrete and reinforced. The old look is to scare people and keep them out."

"It's working," Kelli said.

Jesse smiled and offered his hand. "Let's go see this great mystery."

She took his hand and felt instantly better.

Together, they headed up the mine until Duster didn't make the corner in the mine, but instead just walked through a side wall of the tunnel and vanished.

Both Kellie and Jesse just stopped in their tracks.

"That's just damn mean," Bonnie said as Duster chuckled like a ghost, his laugh echoing down the tunnel.

Kelli was getting damn tired of thinking people were ghosts. First Jesse, now the rest of them.

Suddenly Bonnie appeared from out of the wall.

"One of the many security features," she said. "Hologram."

She stuck her hand back into the wall.

She indicated that they should come with her.

"Close your eyes and just step forward," Bonnie said after they got right next to the wall.

Kelli didn't want to let go of Jesse's hand, but she did so she could put her hand out in front of her as she closed her eyes and stepped toward what looked like a solid wall of rock.

She felt nothing and after a few steps opened her eyes and looked back.

She could see the tunnel, but not where the hologram was.

"That's impressive," Jesse said, glancing back. "I think I'm saying that a lot."

"You haven't seen anything yet," Bonnie said, indicating they should head for the end of the mine. There was no sign of Duster.

"Let me guess," Kelli said, doing her best to keep her nerves under some sort of control. "Another hologram?"

"Got it in one," Bonnie said, laughing.

Jesse and Kelli both followed Bonnie through the second fake wall and into a huge cavern full of racks and racks of period clothing and shelves full of various supplies. Lights hung from the high rock ceiling filled the place with clear light.

Madison and Dawn were standing at one table, working on unpacking their bags.

Duster was at another table seemingly doing the same thing.

Kelli looked over as Jesse stopped beside her.

"I'm starting to think they were telling us the truth," she whispered, her voice lost in the big cavern.

All Jesse could do was nod. Clearly he was feeling the same way.

And that scared her more than she wanted to admit.

CHAPTER SEVENTEEN

July 15th, 2016
Above the ghost town of Silver City, Idaho

JESSE WAS FLAT impressed with all the security features to get into the big supply cavern at the end of an old gold mine. Something was here and clearly they were all prepared, with all the period costumes and period supplies to go back into time, as they had claimed.

He wasn't convinced that was going to happen, but clearly the four of them believed it. And the fact that they did, and he respected all of them, worried him more than he was going to let himself admit at this point.

Bonnie had him and Kelli pack their modern underwear and supplies in hidden compartments of saddlebags.

"These are expensive saddlebags for 1900," Kelli said, glancing over at Bonnie.

"We always travel as people of means," Bonnie said.

"Makes it a ton easier, I'll bet," Kelli said.

"Always," Bonnie said.

After everyone was packed, Dawn said, "Madison and I will fix us all some lunch while you show Jesse and Kelli the cavern and take them on a test run."

With that, Dawn and Madison headed for the back of the cave where Jesse could see a modern kitchen and living area.

"Test run?" Kelli asked, glancing around.

"We'll show you," Bonnie said. "Slip this on."

Jesse watched as Bonnie had Kelli slip on a period dress over her clothes. "No need to button it. It's only in case someone sees us from a distance. We're only going back out front."

Jesse and Duster still wore their long coats and cowboy hats, so they would pass easily in just about any time period.

"Follow me," Duster said.

Jesse glanced at Kelli, who was looking as worried as he felt. But they both followed Duster.

Duster went out of the main cavern into a small tunnel to a door at the back which he unlocked. Then he glanced back at them. "Do not touch the walls."

Then he pushed the door open and went into a well-lit cavern on the other side.

Both Jesse and Kelli got about five steps before they both stopped.

It took Jesse a moment to even begin to understand a part of what he was seeing. The cavern was immense, bigger than most major football stadiums, and one part of it seemed to go off into the distance, sloping downhill.

The floor was flat and seemed to be just dirt and light gray dust. The walls were covered in quartz crystals of some sort.

They had a faint pink look and seemed to radiate power. They were all sizes, from tiny ones growing in clusters to massive ones he couldn't begin to guess size.

His mind would not accept the scale or the size. He felt like an ant.

"Never ceases to take my breath away," Bonnie said.

Duster was standing off to one side slightly, watching Jesse and Kelli.

"Every crystal is the physical representation of a timeline," Duster said. "When you decided to come up here with us, timelines were started off of billions of timelines. We figure this room is just the timelines closest to this timeline."

"Where would the timeline crystals be where we did not come up here?" Kelli asked.

Jesse was impressed that she had asked an intelligent question at all. His mind was still just swirling as he looked around.

"More than likely miles and miles down in that direction somewhere," Duster said, pointing off where the massive cavern just vanished into the distance down into the hill.

Jesse forced himself to clear his mind and look around. About twenty paces from the door, near one wall, was a wooden table with some sort of wooden box on it.

"Is that the machine that allows you to jump into the crystals?" Jesse asked, pointing to the table.

"We are in crystals now," Duster said, nodding. "That allows us to move to another timeline from this one. Nothing more. But this timeline, this crystal we are in, is our home timeline."

"So you are saying that the four of us are at this very moment in all these crystals?" Kelli asked.

"All having this same conversation," Duster nodded.

He turned and headed for the table. "Come on, we'll show you how it works. No risk at all. Just don't touch those walls as I said."

"Energy?" Jesse said.

Duster nodded.

Jesse and Kelli sort of followed Duster and Bonnie like two zombies, both of them doing more staring around them than paying attention to where they were walking.

When they all got near the table, Duster put on gloves, then attached a flexible clamp to one crystal on the wall that looked more like a woman's hair band. Then he attached two wires to the band.

Then he came back over to the box and attached one wire, leaving the other wire from the crystal on the ground for the moment.

Then he adjusted a dial on the wooden box.

"How did you find this place?" Kelli asked.

"We'll tell you all that over lunch," Bonnie said. "For now, when we tell you, just touch the box."

Duster picked up the wire with his gloved hand and connected it to a terminal on the side of the box. Then took his glove off.

"When I say touch, touch the box," Duster said.

He hovered his bare hand over the wooden box and Bonnie did the same.

Jesse and Kelli did the same

"Now," Duster said.

Jesse, at the same time as everyone else, touched the wooden box.

And not a damn thing happened.

Nothing.

CHAPTER EIGHTEEN

October 14th, 1878
Above Silver City, Idaho

"WHAT WENT WRONG?" Kelli asked as Bonnie and Duster stepped back and indicated that she and Jesse do the same.

She glanced around at the massive cavern full of crystals. Nothing had changed as far as she could tell. The box was still hooked up to a crystal on the wall.

"Welcome to 1878," Duster said, turning and heading for the doorway.

"Follow him," Bonnie said.

Kelli turned as Duster got to the big door and opened it. It had been open before. How did it get closed?

"What did he mean by 1878?" Kelli asked.

She couldn't decide if she was just flat stunned by the huge caverns or by all the lack of information. But this was again making her slightly angry.

"Duster sat the machine for October 14th, 1878," Bonnie said as they followed Duster down the short tunnel and back into the big supply cavern. The placed looked a little less crammed with tables and supplies than before.

And the kitchen area where Dawn and Madison had gone was dark. And looked a lot more rustic.

Duster led them back down the mine tunnel toward the entrance.

"Are you saying we are in another timeline now?" Jesse asked. "Or in our own past?"

"We are in another timeline," Bonnie said. "But one so close to our own as to be indistinguishable. So it basically is our own past, yes."

Kelli had no idea what to think of that, so she just said nothing, trying to control the anger she was feeling. Somehow she knew she was being duped. She just didn't understand why or how.

They went the rest of the way down the mine tunnel in silence. Kelli decided she liked the big caverns much more than this narrow mine tunnel, even if Duster and Jesse said it was safe.

At the end, Duster showed them how to look through a big scope to see if anyone was close by.

When Kelli did, what she mostly saw was white. Which made no sense at all to her.

Duster showed them the large button on the wall on the inside that opened the big metal door and slid the rock back. Then he hit it.

The blast of cold air that smashed into Kelli damn near rocked her off her feet. Light blowing snow flew past the opening and a couple inches of snow covered the top of the mine tailings.

When they had come in here, the day was promising to be hot. This wasn't possible.

"I think I'll just go pull the wire," Bonnie said. "Too damn cold for all of us out there for too long.

Duster nodded.

Bonnie stepped back as Duster and Jesse and Kelli moved out into the light blowing snow and the rock slid closed behind them silently.

The intense cold cut through Kelli instantly. She forced herself to look around as much as possible. The old cabin looked brand new and it still had windows and a stove chimney sticking out of the roof.

Duster moved carefully over toward the edge and pointed down.

Jesse took Kelli's hand and they followed Duster.

Kelli felt strength coming from Jesse, even though he had to be feeling the same emotions she was.

When they reached the edge of the mine tailings, down through the light blowing snow they could see the town of Silver City. Only it clearly wasn't a ghost town anymore. There were hundreds of buildings and many of them had lights on and smoke coming from the chimneys.

"Silver City is at its first peak right now," Duster said. "A very rowdy, bustling mining town."

Kelli knew that. And what she was looking at looked exactly like the pictures of Silver City in its prime. Only covered in inches of snow.

"So we are really in 1878?" Jesse asked.

"Yes," Duster said. "I'll explain how my family got this mine and how we built all those security features in this time over lunch."

Kelli looked around, trying not to shiver so hard she would lose her grip on Jesse's hand. Through the light snow she could see dozens of other mines and some of the shacks on the tops of the tailings had lights in them.

"We're going to need to get inside," Jesse said.

"We will," Duster said. "When Bonnie pulls a wire off the machine, the connection to this timeline will be broken and we'll return to the cavern in our own timeline."

Kelli was about to say, "Soon, I hope." But the words never got out of her mouth.

She found herself standing next to Bonnie and Jesse and Duster touching the wooden box on the table. Around her the massive cavern covered in crystals glowed.

But she was still shivering and colder than she could remember being in a very long time. And she had only been out there for a very short period of time.

Duster and Bonnie both stepped back and turned and headed for the open door.

"Come on," Bonnie said, smiling at Jesse and Kelli. "Dawn and Madison will have some hot chocolate waiting."

"Damn I hope so," Kelli muttered as, shivering, she followed them.

She wasn't completely sure if the shivering was from the cold or the shock of just having traveled in time.

CHAPTER NINETEEN

July 15th, 2016
Above the ghost town of Silver City, Idaho

JESSE FELT LIKE he sort of stumbled from the crystal cavern and into the storage area and then to the modern kitchen in a back corner. He had his coat on and still felt chilled. He couldn't imagine how Kelli was feeling.

The kitchen looked like it had been transplanted from a modern home and stuck in a back corner of a cave. A wood-like flooring, tan granite counters, wood-stained cabinets, a modern metallic stove and fridge.

The center of the area had a large wooden table with eight padded chairs around it that matched the décor. On the other side of the table from the kitchen counters was a living room like area with two large couches and a number of over-stuff chairs with reading lamps.

Bathroom's in the back," Dawn said, pointing to a small tunnel that led off the kitchen area.

She had hot chocolate on three spots on the table and pointed to two chairs on the living room side of the table.

"Sandwiches and a salad will be ready shortly."

Jesse really wanted to ask how they got all this into the cavern without being seen, but his mind wasn't really working. So he just sat down where Dawn pointed, leaving on his coat, and wrapped his hands around the ceramic mug of hot chocolate.

The smell was wonderful and helped bring him back to his mind, even though it was far too warm to drink.

Bonnie tossed a bag of mini-marshmallows in front of Duster, then took her cup of hot chocolate and sat down next to him on the kitchen side.

"Did that really just happen?" Kelli asked.

Jesse was impressed. A far more logical question than he could form at the moment.

"It did," Duster said, nodding as he put marshmallows in his mug. "We took you back into a snowstorm to not only make it clear about what happened, but to show you the town below."

"So the picture wasn't fake," Jesse said, trying to grasp what had happened. "All four of us end up, at some point in the future, standing in Roosevelt in 1908."

Duster and Bonnie both nodded.

"At least the four of us from another timeline," Bonnie said. "We can't go back into our own timeline. We are blocked from that, even if we could find which crystal is this timeline. And we are blocked from going back into any timeline when we are alive in that timeline, so we can't go back and talk with ourselves."

"So we can't just go back five years," Kelli said.

Duster and Bonnie nodded.

Jesse glanced at the silver bracelet he was wearing. "That's why I can be wearing this bracelet in the picture."

Again Bonnie and Duster nodded.

"So how much time have you spent in the past of other timelines?" Kelli asked.

Jesse looked up from his wrist at the silence.

Both Bonnie and Duster were looking at each other and Dawn and Bonnie had their backs turned and were working on lunch. Jesse had no doubt that question was a hard one to answer.

Finally, Duster started off the answer. "The mathematics of all this allow us to only be gone from this timeline for exactly two minutes and fifteen seconds."

"It took us ten minutes to get out there and freeze our asses," Jesse said. So the two minute number made no sense.

"We spent ten minutes or so in that timeline," Bonnie said. "But in this timeline you only aged just over two minutes."

"So why two minutes and fifteen seconds?" Kelli asked.

"It's the math of how that works," Bonnie said. "Very complex, but it never varies."

"So how did we get to Roosevelt in 1908?" Jesse asked and suddenly Kelli was nodding in agreement to his question.

"We rode horseback," Duster said. "Takes about four days from here."

Jesse stared at Duster, then glanced at Kelli, who was staring at Duster with her mouth open.

Bonnie smiled. "Let me be clear. We can go into another timeline, be part of that timeline, age in that timeline, even

grow old or die, or be killed in that timeline, and when we are done, only two minutes and fifteen seconds have passed here."

Silence filled the cavern. Jesse had no idea what to say to that.

"So answer my first question," Kelli said to Duster and Bonnie. "How much time have you spent in the past?"

Duster shrugged and glanced at Bonnie.

"It adds up fast," Bonnie said. "I stopped counting after the first few thousand years."

Dawn put a salad on the table. "I'm still counting. We have known about this place for a couple years now real time, as we call it. And because of the weather, we can only come up here in the summer. We have spent just over seventeen hundred years in the past."

"And died in the past?" Jesse asked, trying to get his mind around any of this.

"I died on my first major trip back," Madison said. "Maybe four other times since, once of old age."

"And you end up back here, alive, with only just over two minutes passed?"

Dawn and Duster and Bonnie all nodded.

"Holy shit," Jesse said.

It was the only damn thing he could think to say.

CHAPTER TWENTY

July 15th, 2016
Above the ghost town of Silver City, Idaho

KELLI WORKED AT a wonderful ham sandwich with cheese spread with a mustard that had a bite to it. The idea that she could live a long time in the past without aging just had stunned her into silence.

So finally, after halfway through lunch, Duster brought up the Season Medals she had been trying to track.

"We tend to always go back on the first trips with everyone," Duster said. "Show you the ropes of living and existing in the past."

Kelli nodded.

"So you up for doing some research on the Season Medals," Duster asked, "and the guy Bushnell, with us tagging along?"

That stunned her. She almost asked about the helicopter coming back at four when she realized that with each trip only taking two minutes, she could spend hundreds and hundreds of years in the past and they could still catch that flight back to Boise.

She flat didn't know what to say. She really couldn't grasp the idea that if she went back into the past, she could live and grow old in another timeline and just have two minutes pass here.

But beside her Jesse seemed to be doing a little better in getting his feet under him after all this.

"Kelli," he said, looking at her. "I would love to help on the investigation of the crime. I'm a trained investigator and pretty good at my job. I might be able to help you as well."

She looked up into those wonderful green eyes of his and realized that she wanted him to help. She wanted to get to know him a lot better.

And she really wanted to understand this gift Duster and Bonnie were offering her out of nowhere. If what they were saying even came close to being on target, the value to her research and her books would be off the charts.

But she needed to know a couple more details.

"Is it possible to change the past?"

"In another timeline," Duster said, "sure."

"When we go back into another timeline, we are part of that timeline," Bonnie said. "If you had kids in that timeline, they would still be there if you came back here. Your actions change that timeline."

"But how can you go back if you have lived that long in the past?" Jesse asked. "There are only so many years available back there if you can't be in the same timeline at the same time."

"That's correct," Duster said. "Say we jumped to 1908. Bonnie and I have lived through 1908 more times than I care to think about. But if we jumped back there now, we would just arrive in a timeline where we had not been before."

"Remember," Bonnie said, "there are more billions of timelines than we can imagine, all basically identical to this one, and by us picking a date to go back, we split off a new timeline at the moment we arrive by the very choice."

"Oh," was all Jesse said.

Kelli was just trying to imagine investigating a crime in the past. She would have to back up anything she found in the past with modern references. But she could do that.

She turned to Jesse and looked into his green eyes. "You up for helping me with investigation into a possible murder in the past? And tracking some medals?"

He smiled. "I would love to."

She turned to Bonnie and Duster. "When are we leaving?"

Both Bonnie and Duster were smiling.

"How about as soon as April and Ryan get here," Duster said. "Which should be any moment now. They are driving in from Boise. They left before we arrived from Portland."

"April and Ryan?" Kelli asked.

"April is a historical interior designer and Ryan is an architect," Jesse said.

"We want to build the lodge again," Madison said, laughing. "If we're going to spend a decade or so in the Roosevelt area, we might as well be comfortable."

Kelli looked at Dawn and Madison, then at Bonnie and Duster. "How often have you built the lodge?"

All of them but Dawn shrugged.

"This will be the twenty-second time," Dawn said, smiling.

Duster laughed. "That means it exists in a hell of a lot of timelines now, that's for sure."

Kelli once again had nothing she could say.

PART THREE
The Trail

CHAPTER TWENTY-ONE

July 9th, 1906
Oregon Coast

JESSE NUDGED HIS horse up a slight rise in the wide trail that wound through thick old-growth pine above the rocks and pounding surf of the Pacific Ocean below him. The air was brisk with a slight wind coming off the waves a hundred feet below, bringing the wonderful surf smells and the feeling that the air was so fresh, it should be bottled.

Sometimes the trails that wound along the coast were downright scary as they skirted near cliff edges and up and down steep grades. The ground along the ocean always seemed to be wet and muddy, even in the summer. This trail was just far enough into the shade of the old trees that it thankfully didn't feel dangerous.

Jesse reached the top of the slight rise and glanced back as Kelli expertly climbed the trail on her horse. He might look like a cowboy more than she did, but she clearly was a better rider than he had become. Over the last year in the past, they had both become fine riders. She just seemed to have a natural talent for being in control of a horse.

He had on his standard jeans, thick cotton shirt, and long duster coat. His matching cowboy hat and worn leather boots completed his look.

Kelli had on women's riding clothes of this time, with leather-like dark-brown pants, a blouse with a leather jacket-like tan vest, and a wide-brimmed tan hat that she kept tied to her head with a strap under her chin. Both of them had saddlebags and travel bags strapped behind them, plus saddle rifles in holsters near their right legs.

Over the last year they had both also become great shots, mostly for safety in chasing away animals they ran across. Neither of them had any desire at all to hunt or kill anything.

She also had started wearing cowboy boots and actually admitted she liked them after a year now in the past. "Not as good as my tennis shoes, but not bad."

He stopped and eased his horse to the outside of a wide area in the trail to let her come up beside him.

"Can you imagine," he said, "I was following you right about here just yesterday in 2016? And we hadn't met yet."

She shook her head, smiling at him. "I can't seem to wrap my mind around the fact that this entire trip, all this time, this entire last year in the past, will only take just over two minutes in our timeline."

He laughed. "I find it amazing that it has only been a day since we met."

"Longest damn day I have ever spent," she said.

"I hope that's in a good way."

She laughed. "Jury is still out on that."

Then she eased her horse forward, moving on along the trail ahead of him. So once again he was following her into Whale Port, Oregon.

Could history repeat itself when the repeating came over a hundred years before the first event? Sometimes this time travel stuff just gave him a headache.

If he and Kelli had done their investigation correctly, John Simon Bushnell would be arriving in the small town overland sometime in the next two days. They wanted to be there to see him and follow him on to Roosevelt, Idaho.

Jesse stayed a few horse lengths behind Kelli along the trail as it turned inland away from the ocean and widened slightly. He vaguely remembered the future highway in 2016 doing the same thing at this point.

The day that Duster and Bonnie had shown them the mine had really been something. Even though they had taken him out into a snowstorm on the first jump into the past, Jesse just couldn't imagine actually going and living in the past.

Then, after April and Ryan arrived at the cavern and were introduced around, they all started to work to pack. Bonnie helped Jesse and Kelli make sure they had what they would need. And Duster showed them both the stash of gold and money and got them both situated with enough money to survive in style in the past.

Duster had promised them both that later on he would teach them how to make money by going into the past. But he hadn't done that yet in this first year.

Then, with all eight of them in the crystal cavern, which was even more mind-numbing the second time, Duster and Madison and Dawn and April and Ryan had all touched the box and vanished.

That had stunned Jesse down to his core. It was not every day you saw five people just vanish in front of you.

Kelli had just grabbed his hand for comfort.

With a glove on, Bonnie quickly adjusted the time on the machine and at the count of three, they all touched the wooden box with a bare hand, jumping into the past and into the same timeline as the other five had gone into less than fifteen seconds behind the others.

Again, the movement into the other timeline had been no event as far as Jesse was concerned. It felt like nothing had happened.

But supposedly the other five had gone back in the timeline to the spring of 1899 to build homes in Boise and get ready to build the big Lodge starting the summer of 1900. They planned on building the lodge and having it open by the spring of 1902.

In 1903 they were also going to build a home in Roosevelt down the valley from the lodge that they could all use at different times while there.

Kelli's research on the Season Medals and Bushnell didn't start until 1907, so they had decided that going back to the summer of 1906 would be enough time ahead for them.

Jesse couldn't imagine that Duster and the others had lived for almost seven years at that point, but when Duster had greeted Bonnie and him and Kelli in the supply cavern, it was clear he had. He looked older and a little more worn.

And he was very happy to see Bonnie.

For him it had been seven years since he had seen his wife, but only fifteen seconds had passed for Jesse and Bonnie and Kelli.

Duster had brought them horses and supplies and they all headed slowly toward Boise.

It had taken both Jesse and Kelli some days to finally totally believe they were actually in 1906. And it took them those same days to get used to riding horses again. They had done a lot of walking early on.

Jesse and Kelli had spent that summer in a number of places. Sometimes they had been up at the wonderful Monumental Summit Lodge, enjoying the crystal clear air and night skies full of so many stars, it was hard to imagine. They had also spent a week down in the mining boomtown of Roosevelt to get used to the town. Then they had gone into Boise as the late summer weather started to change.

Jesse and Kelli then had spent the winter of 1906/1907 in Boise in Bonnie and Duster's wonderful mansion there, in two guest rooms, mostly just learning how to be comfortable with living in the past and also planning the investigation the next year.

They had spent some time in the Boise library and in the archives of the Idaho Statesman pouring over past papers to find more information.

On about the sixth day in the past, while sitting on the deck overlooking the

NUMBER FIFTEEN
DECEMBER, 2014

Smith's MONTHLY

Original Stories, Novels, and Articles

DEAN WESLEY SMITH

COLD CALL
A Cold Poker Gang Novel

Don't Miss an Issue!
Subscribe
Electronic Subscription:
6 Issues... $29.99
12 Issues... $49.99

Paper Subscription:
6 Issues... $59.99
12 Issues... $99.99

For Full
Subscription Information
Go To:
www.SmithsMonthly.com

Monumental Valley, Jesse and Kelli had both acknowledged to each other their growing attraction and desire to have a relationship with each other. But they had both decided to just wait until the time was right to take it any farther.

At that point they both felt very out of place living in 1906 and any complication just seemed like too much.

Living in Bonnie and Duster's home did not allow that time to be right at any point over the winter either. The flirting between the two of them had reached wonderful levels as far as Jesse was concerned. And they had spent many an evening walking hand-in-hand along the Boise River talking and getting to know each other better.

And they had talked about many different possible investigations they could do together. He loved the idea of using his investigative skills to unearth historical crimes and solve them and Kelli loved his help.

It had been a fantastic year.

And now they were finally on the Season Medals trail. As Kelli had said, "They were finally on the case."

If they could actually discover what happened to Bushnell and what happened to the Season Medals he had acquired from the Native Americans, Kelli could write a fantastic book.

And if they did manage to figure out what happened to the medals and then recover them in 2016, they planned on giving them to museums and back to their tribes. Since neither of them needed money, that seemed like the best idea. Jesse flat loved that idea.

When they had told Bonnie and Duster about that idea over dinner one night, the two of them had just beamed. It seemed the idea of doing something like

that was one of the reasons they helped historians.

Now, less than one actual real-time day since they had met, but a year in past time, they were again approaching Whale Port, Oregon.

But now, instead of in modern cars, they were on horseback.

And for Jesse, after a year in the past, that now just seemed natural.

CHAPTER TWENTY-TWO

July 9th, 1906
Oregon Coast

AHEAD THROUGH THE trees, Kelli could see the small coast fishing village of Whale Port.

She glanced over her shoulder at Jesse. "Following me again?"

"I am," he said, smiling at her with that wonderful smile she had grown to love. "And with pleasure."

He had to be the most handsome man she had ever met. And smart and kind and gentle.

"Twice could be considered stalking you know," she said.

"Not sure if that term is even used that way in this time period," he said, laughing.

She got her horse down and through a stream coming off the side of the hill and headed toward the town. From what she could see, Whale Port hadn't changed much in the hundred-plus years. The hotel sat majestically on a slight bluff looking out over the ocean. Unlike in 2016, no other buildings had yet been built next to it.

Painted bright white, the hotel had two round towers on the two front corners that made it seem larger and taller than its three stories. She hoped like hell she would see the view from those towers shortly.

She could also see the restaurant where she and Jesse had met. It still looked the same, only without a paved parking lot. A wooden boardwalk that ran about two blocks connected the shops and restaurant and hotel. Horse ties lined the boardwalk.

There were very few horses tied up at any point along the boardwalk.

The main road, that in the future would become the coast highway, was just a mud wagon road. The new cars that dotted Boise in 1906, and startled horses, had not made it over here yet. She doubted there was any way to get a car over the coast range and here.

There was also a general store, and on the side of town closest to where they were coming in was a stable. On the far side of town and out of sight, she knew a wide wagon road ran down to docks on the small inlet.

A wagon road also led up into the hills and eventually to Portland. But from here it was a lot easier to take a ship out and into the Columbia River and up to Portland.

She and Jesse had decided to take the longer route to get here. They had taken a train from Boise to Portland and then down the Willamette Valley to Salem. The ride had been wonderful, but very bumpy, and they both had berths so small one person could barely turn around in it. So they had spent most of their time in the dining car, eating and drinking coffee and enjoying the time talking.

In Salem, they had bought two horses and headed for the coast. The ride from Salem over the Coastal Mountain Range

to a small town called Taft had taken them two days, stopping in the small town of Grand Ronde on the first night.

From there they had gone north up the coast, sometimes having to wait for low tide to use the beach as a trail, other times following a wagon road through the trees inland. The ride up the coast had taken three more days, stopping in two small hotels along the way.

She glanced back at the handsome man behind her again, but he seemed to be looking out over the ocean at the spectacular blue waters and light waves.

Even though they had known each other for less than a day in their real timeline, they had been in the past for a year and still hadn't slept together. It seemed that finding privacy in 1906 was not an easy thing to do, especially when not officially a couple and living in the home of two close friends all winter. Plus Boise was a town that valued propriety of its wealthy.

Something about screaming and moaning just down the hallway in Bonnie and Duster's home would be too embarrassing to talk about at breakfast. And she had a hunch that once she and Jesse got started, there would be a lot of both screaming in pleasure and moaning in delight.

Even without the Humpty Dumpty sex, she had really enjoyed her time with Jesse, the walks along the river, the wonderful planning sessions. But if she didn't jump his body pretty soon, there was going to be hell to pay.

So tonight she was going to change up how they traveled. Instead of traveling together as two people of means, she wanted Jesse to sign them in as a married couple and get the largest suite in the hotel if it was available.

They had met here, why not take their relationship to the next level here?

Besides, they planned on staying here for some time, waiting for Bushnell to show up. So why not make the best of the time.

And sex with a handsome, smart man, seemed like a damn good use of her time.

CHAPTER TWENTY-THREE

July 9th, 1906
Oregon Coast

IT DIDN'T TAKE them long to get the horses into the stable and start down the boardwalk with their saddlebags over their shoulders. Kelli also carried a carpetbag in her hand and he carried two small satchel-like bags, one hers, one his.

"Let's change this up," she said, smiling at him as they walked toward the diner and the white hotel beyond. The sounds of the ocean below the town seemed to almost pause for a moment as she stared at him.

He frowned. What in the world was she talking about?

She pulled a gold band from her pocket and held it up. "Bonnie lent this to me."

His heart skipped a beat he was sure. Either that or the world just stopped for a moment.

She stopped, put her bag down on the sidewalk, and as he watched, she slipped the gold band on her wedding finger and held her hand up. "How about we sign up as a married couple and take this relationship up a step?"

Damn he liked that idea. He had been thinking about that very thing himself.

"But we've only known each other for less than a day," he said, smiling at her.

"I've had quicker," she said, smiling back as she picked up her bag and they kept heading for the hotel.

"That sounds like a fun story for later," he said, grinning at her. "So am I Mr. Rae or are you Mrs. Parks?"

"Since this is 1906," she said, "lets be traditional. But we can switch off as we go along."

"Kinky, Mrs. Parks," he said.

She laughed and at that moment the smell of fresh baking bread hit them both.

They both turned like someone had pulled their strings and stared at the restaurant. It didn't look like it had any customers at all.

"Feels to me like we have flashed back to 2016," she said, taking a deep breath of the thick-smelling air.

Jesse was almost sure he could taste the bread and how it would melt in his mouth.

"I think I'm going to be hungry sooner than later," he said. "Amazing."

They somehow kept on going down the boardwalk past the front of the restaurant, even though doing that felt difficult at best for Jesse.

But Duster and Bonnie had trained them well. A person of means in this time would get checked into their room first, then freshen up, change clothes, and go out for dinner. Even in a small town on the Oregon Coast they needed to maintain their image.

The four stone steps in front of the hotel led up from the boardwalk and through two open large wooden doors. Inside, the lobby had high ceilings with a large crystal chandelier hanging down in the very middle.

A massive smooth-rock fireplace dominated one wall of the lobby and the windows were a good fifteen feet tall, letting in a lot of the afternoon light.

The floors were polished pine and area carpets were under some dark brown overstuffed couches and chairs to one side. One wall near the fireplace was filled with books on what looked like dark cedar shelving.

"Those look interesting," Kelli whispered, nodding toward the shelves of books.

"Are you saying with all the sex you'll have time to read?" he whispered back.

"God, I hope not," she said, laughing.

There was no one in the lobby at all except for a man behind the main wooden desk at the far wall, but Jesse had a hunch that on rainy days, this large room would serve as a gathering place for town locals to sit, read the papers, and talk around the fire.

Jesse immediately felt at home here. He wasn't sure why, but he could feel himself relax a little as he moved across the lobby, placed the bags beside a large wooden column and moved toward the front desk.

"This is really nice," he heard Kelli say behind him.

The man in a suit and tie and vest nodded and bowed slightly. "Welcome."

The guy looked almost out of place in the suit. His face was weathered and tanned dark from far too much time in the sun and weather. Clearly before taking this job he must have been on a fishing boat, or he had worked as a logger.

"Jesse Parks," Jesse said, reaching out his hand.

The man took it and shook it and again bowed slightly. Clearly that man knew he was facing a couple of means.

"My wife and I," Jesse said, glancing back at Kelli who smiled, "would like your best suite for upwards of a week."

"We have that available," the man said, nodding and turning for the key to the room.

He slid the key to Jesse, then asked him to sign the big black register book that was open on the counter.

Jesse signed Mr. and Mrs. Parks, which felt very strange. He didn't mind it. It just felt strange.

Then he noticed the name two above his own, and also dated today.

John Simon Bushnell.

Bushnell was already here.

Their research had been off just slightly. Nothing to worry about. At least Bushnell was here.

Jesse slid the man behind the desk enough money to cover the room for the week. "Please put any extra on the account and we can settle at the end of our stay."

"As you wish, sir," the man said, opening a drawer and putting the cash away quickly. "I will leave a receipt in your letter box."

"That would be fine," Jesse said, nodding.

"Would you like me to help with your luggage?" the man asked.

"Thank you, but no," Jesse said. "We are traveling light this trip to the coast, so I think we will be fine."

"The suite is on the third floor," the man said, nodding. "Simply turn right at the top of the stairs. First door on the right. The room is named Shipside."

"We'll find it fine," Jesse said. Then he slipped the man a decent tip and turned for the luggage.

With Kelli leading up the wide, white-painted staircase with a dark maroon carpet runner down the middle, they headed to their suite.

On the third floor he handed Kelli the key.

"Aren't you supposed to carry me across the threshold?" she asked, smiling at him.

"I'll get you over more than enough thresholds later," he said, smiling.

"Damn that sounds wonderful," she said, pretending to fan herself before turning and opening the door to the suite.

And it did sound wonderful. He just hoped Bushnell's early arrival wouldn't mess things up.

CHAPTER TWENTY-FOUR

July 9th, 1906
Oregon Coast

KELLI WAS STUNNED as she opened the suite door and walked in. The place felt very, very familiar in a way she couldn't quickly place.

The massive tall windows looked out over the Pacific Ocean and gave the room a feeling as if the room were built on a patio. A stone fireplace dominated the wall to the left going all the way up to the tall ceilings and the corner of the room extended out into the round tower.

All the windows in the tower and along the ocean side of the building were tall and the brown drapes were pulled aside on all of them letting in a massive amount of light.

The floor was polished pine with brown area carpets under two dark-colored couches and three large chairs grouped in front of the fireplace. A light-wood table with five chairs with cushion pads on the seats sat in the round area of the room. That would be a stunning place to work and eat breakfast and plan.

To the right was a large bedroom with a huge bed and open closet next to a dresser. Beyond that Kelli could see a bathroom.

"Wow," Jesse said, as he put the bags down and closed the door, looking around.

Suddenly she remembered why this was familiar. "This is patterned after the Idanha Hotel suites in Boise," Kelli said. "One day, while Bonnie and I were in the downtown Boise area, she wanted to show me the suites there for times when we came back and needed a place to stay. But those suite sure didn't have this view."

She moved over and stood staring out at the ocean. The swells were gentle and the sun was still fairly high in the sky. Only a few wispy white clouds littered the sky.

From where she stood, she could see the muddy street in front of the hotel and the boardwalk, from where it ended in the road down to the docks to where it went to the stables on the other side of town.

But at the moment, it wasn't the view of the small town that had her attention, but the vivid blue ocean and lighter blue sky as far as she could see.

Jesse came over and put his arms around her. "Pretty special place."

"Let's make it special," she said, turning and kissing him.

They had kissed before, but it has always been guarded kisses. This one, for both of them was a full-on passionate kiss.

And after a moment they both came up for air.

His face was flushed and she knew hers was as well. She could feel the heat and the passion.

She then kissed him again, almost as hard and for almost as long.

Then she pushed away and said, "I have to get out of these clothes and cleaned up."

With that, she turned and started taking off clothes as she headed into the bedroom.

She managed to get out of her riding coat and her blouse, leaving only her modern sports bra on before she asked for help with her boots.

He had managed to get out of his duster, his shirt, and had his pants unbuttoned and his belt loose.

He came over to her as she dropped onto the colorful quilts covering the soft featherbed. She lay on her back and put her feet up in the air.

He eased off one of her boots, then the other one.

"Now help with these pants, would you?"

She unbuttoned her pants and had him pull them off her, leaving only her blue modern underwear on.

Then she pointed at his pants. "Get those off."

She slipped out of her sports bra and underwear and sat there on the featherbed watching him get his boots off and then his pants and then his underwear.

She just stared at him, stunned at how wonderfully he was built and how his muscles in his back seemed to ripple as he moved.

Then he turned and stared at her.

He was clearly aroused and the most handsome man she had ever seen with or without clothes.

"You are so beautiful," he said, moving to her and pushing her back on the bed and kissing her.

His skin felt wonderful against her and she pushed against him.

It was as if electricity was holding them together.

He pushed back.

And frantically they worked at doing what they had both wanted to do for some time.

And if there was screaming in ecstasy or moaning in satisfaction that alarmed the neighbors, or even the fish down in the ocean, she flat didn't care.

It was just so damn good.

CHAPTER TWENTY-FIVE

July 9th, 1906
Oregon Coast

JESSE LAY BESIDE Kelli, his head propped on his hand watching her naked chest heave up and down as if she had just run a fast mile. He felt the same way completely.

That had been fast and intense.

He stroked her chest and then let his hand move down her stomach to rest there.

"Sorry that was so fast," he said, laughing. "After a year of lusting after your wonderful body and flirting and fleeting kisses and falling for that wonderful brain of yours, it's amazing I didn't explode when you took your blouse off."

She laughed. "I think I had my first orgasm looking at you standing there naked."

He kissed her again, and she turned and pressed into him.

And once again he pressed back.

And this time he took much longer, and it was even better than the first time, if that was possible.

They just fit together in so many, many ways.

After they finished yet again, she looked up, her dark eyes intense. "This is better than I had imagined," she said. "And I imagined some pretty intense stuff over the last year."

"That's what that noise was coming down the hall at night at Bonnie and Duster's," he said.

She laughed and kissed him, then said, "It might have been."

"So how about we get cleaned up like a proper couple and see if the food in that restaurant is as good as it was in 2016?"

"I would love that," she said.

She rolled out of the bed and headed for the bathroom. He watched her go, hoping beyond hope that this would be something he would watch for many years to come.

She stopped in the bathroom door and looked back. "You coming?"

"Admiring the wonderful view."

"Well," she said, turning and facing him completely naked. "Get in here and admire it while we get cleaned up. After that many orgasms, you have to feed a lady."

With that, he joined her.

Thirty minutes later, they again looked like a 1906 couple of means as they left their suite.

As they were headed down the stairs, he realized what he had forgotten to tell her.

"In all the excitement," he said, keeping his voice low so it wouldn't carry, "I forgot to mention to you that Bushnell signed in right ahead of us."

She nodded, then said, keeping her voice low as well. "So our timing was off by a day or so. But he's supposed to have stayed here for five days."

"So we have time to get eyes on him," Jesse said. "That's what I figured."

"I just wish we knew what he was doing here for those days," Kelli said.

"That's what we're going to find out," Jesse said. "If we can stay out of bed long enough to follow him."

"So what we did was exciting?" she asked, smiling up at him as they reached the still-empty lobby and headed for the front doors.

"I would call it more mind-blowing amazing," he said, giving her hand a squeeze.

"You really know how to sweet-talk a girl, don't you?"

"You're the writer," he said, laughing. "Come up with a better description."

"Nope," she said, squeezing his hand back as they went out into the warm summer evening on the Oregon Coast. "I think mind-blowing amazing described it just perfectly."

CHAPTER TWENTY-SIX

July 9th, 1906
Oregon Coast

IT WAS STUNNING how little the restaurant had changed in 2016 from its original look now. Stools were gone, but tall chairs were tucked up against a wooden-covered bar. The booths weren't there, instead were tables with checkered tablecloths and wooden chairs.

But the shape remained the same, the kitchen was in the same place, only closed off more, and the floors were pine instead of a new tile.

And the smell in the restaurant was to die for. Sizzling steak smell added into frying fish and baked bread. Kelli had no idea just how hungry she was until Jesse opened that restaurant door for her.

A small woman with red hair moved toward them with a wide smile on her face that made her freckles stand out.

"Welcome," she said, bowing slightly.

"Table for two," Jesse said and the woman indicated a table against the front window looking out over the ocean. Kelli would never get used to that stunning view. She could just stare at it for hours at a time.

As Jesse held the chair for her and then went around the table to take off his coat and hang it up with his hat, Kelli glanced up at a man eating alone two tables away.

Just as she had recognized Jesse in a picture, she knew instantly that was Bushnell.

He was balding, with light gray at the temples of his short brown hair. He wore the standard suit coat and vest and tie of the time, all shades of dark gray. He had a short dark overcoat hanging on a hook beside his chair with brown leather saddlebags hanging on another hook.

Since he had checked into the hotel, it was more than likely what was in those saddlebags was something he didn't want stolen from his hotel room, and that he didn't trust to a small town hotel safe.

The saddlebags seemed to have a bulk to them. She had no doubt that thirty Season Medals, if individually wrapped, would have bulk to them. Each Season Medal was about the size around of a thin small doughnut, made mostly of silver. Thirty of them wrapped up would have weight, she had no doubt.

She was very happy to see that. It meant he had not lost them at this point in his travels.

As Jesse pulled his chair forward to the table and took his napkin from the table and spread it on his lap, Kelli leaned forward and whispered, "Bushnell is two tables behind you. He has a very heavy-looking saddlebag with him."

Jesse nodded and smiled. Then he stood to pretend to get something from his coat pocket. As he did, he glanced toward Bushnell.

Then he sat back down and nodded. "Looks like we are finally getting started."

She gave him smile. "On more than one thing."

She loved that he blushed slightly as he smiled. How she had been so lucky as to find a man this handsome, this smart, was beyond her. She really, really owed Bonnie and Duster a huge thank-you for sending him to investigate her.

And if she had her way, he would investigate even more of her later.

The thought made her laugh and Jesse frowned.

She waved her hand. "Just imagining what we are going to do later."

He smiled. "Oh, trust me, it will be fun and feel great, but it won't be a laughing matter."

"Now I like the sounds of that promise," she said.

And she did. More than she wanted to admit.

CHAPTER TWENTY-SEVEN

July 9th, 1906
Oregon Coast

BUSHNELL FINISHED UP his dinner and then paid while Jesse and Kelli were still finishing their first course. So as Bushnell put on his coat, Jesse excused himself from Kelli.

As he stood, leaving his coat and hat on the hook, he apologized loud enough for Bushnell to hear.

"I'll be right back, dear," he said. "I just needed to get something from our room."

Kelli nodded and smiled, "Don't be too long, dear. I would hate for your meal to chill."

Jesse smiled at her and went out the door, walking down the wide board-walk at a normal pace toward the hotel. The evening air was still clean and crisp and comfortable, with almost no breeze off the ocean. The sun was still a couple hours above the horizon.

About halfway to the hotel, Jesse heard the door to the restaurant close behind him.

He glanced back to see Bushnell following him with the heavy saddlebag over his shoulder. Kelli had been right. That bag had a heft to it, there was no doubt. To someone in this time period who knew what they were looking for, that bag was like a sign for Bushnell to be robbed. He carried it like he had pounds of gold in there.

Jesse went into the hotel and moved off to one side of the lobby, picking up a local paper and pretending to read intently as Bushnell came in.

Jesse let Bushnell get up to the first floor before he went across the lobby and up the stairs himself. Bushnell hadn't even looked around, but instead walked with his eyes on the floor in front of him.

Bushnell stopped on the second floor and Jesse could hear him from his heavy steps on the wood floor turn down the hallway to the right.

Jesse reached the second floor just as Bushnell opened the third door down the hallway from the stairwell and went in-

side and closed it. The sound of the bolt latching from the inside echoed in the hallway.

Jesse turned around and headed back down the stairs, again going to the newspaper near one seating area and pretending to read.

After five minutes, when Bushnell hadn't come down, Jesse put the paper down and returned to the restaurant just as the waitress was serving his steak, still sizzling.

And beside the steak was a cob of corn and a large dinner roll. Perfect, and it smelled heavenly.

"Any luck?" Kelli asked.

Jesse smiled as he picked up his fork and knife. "A beautiful woman and a wonderful meal. Can't get much luckier than that."

She shook her head. "Trust me, mister. You're going to get a lot luckier later."

"Does that mean I should eat fast?" he asked, looking intently into her dark eyes.

"No," she said, shaking her head as she dug at her corn with a knife as a woman should do in this time period. "I would rather have you eat and build up your strength."

"Same goes for you," he said, laughing.

And then he leaned forward and whispered, "Our target is tucked in bed on the second floor, third room down on the right."

"So we have until dawn," she said, nodding.

"I would love to make the best of that time in more ways than just one."

She laughed as she took a spoonful of corn. "I can think of about a dozen ways."

He really, really liked the sound of that.

The First Four Seeders Universe Novels
Available at your favorite booksellers.

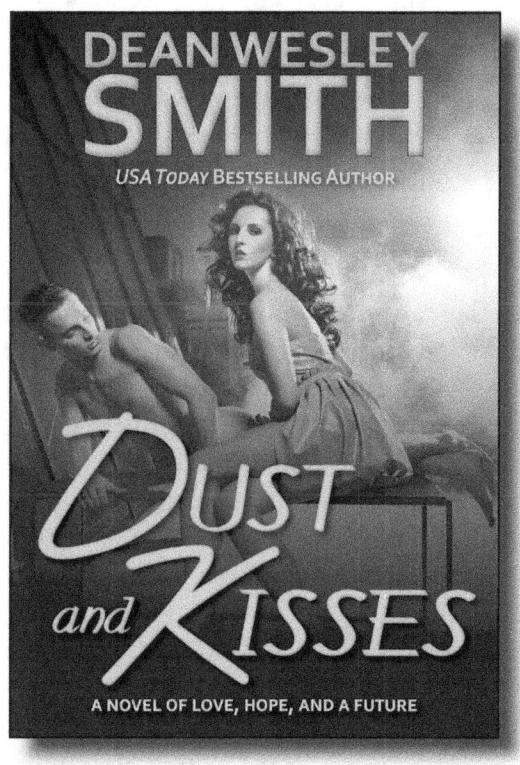

CHAPTER TWENTY-EIGHT

July 9th, 1906
Oregon Coast

AT DAWN, BOTH Kelli and Jesse were dressed and ready to move if they had to. It had been a wonderful night in the large featherbed, making love and then holding each other and sleeping together.

But as the sun came up, they got cleaned up and got focused back on the reason they were in this wonderful hotel overlooking the ocean in the first place.

Kelli set up her notes and stuff at the table in the round corner of the room. From there, even though the sun was still hours from clearing the coastal range and hitting the street of the town below, she could see everything.

Jesse went in search of a back way out of the hotel to make sure Bushnell didn't sneak out on them for any reason. There was a back door, but it simply led around and back to the boardwalk. Directly behind the hotel was a rock cliff that didn't look easy to climb, and a forest above the cliff.

His first impression about the town in 2016 was right. It really was just perched on a ledge between the mountains and the ocean.

Since the hotel had no room service or restaurant, Jesse then went to the restaurant, waving slightly at Kelli from the restaurant door. He couldn't see her through the window, but he knew she was there.

He ordered them both massive fresh rolls, a large pot of fresh-brewed coffee, and some of the most amazing-looking cookies he had ever seen. It would hold them until lunch and he promised to bring the coffeepot back for a refill at lunch.

Then he headed back to the hotel.

"I couldn't see you from the restaurant," he said. "And the only way out the back forces anyone back onto the boardwalk."

Kelli nodded. "Great."

She was dressed in her riding clothes since it seemed a number of women in this town dressed that way normally. A city dress made no sense here. She was alternating between her notes and watching out the window and seemed distracted.

"I just can't figure out why Bushnell is here," she said as he spread out the large rolls that smelled wonderful, like a cross between a bun and a modern cinnamon roll.

"A meeting," Jesse said as he poured her a cup of coffee. "An isolated place like this would be perfect for a meeting."

She nodded. "But usually Bushnell went to the people he wanted to meet."

Jesse sat down and pointed in the direction of the small harbor just out of sight at the north end of the town. "Maybe that's exactly what he is doing here."

Kelli frowned, then looked up at him. "I have been thinking about this wrong. Damn it all."

Jesse stared at her, sort of surprised. They had gone over this a few times before leaving Boise and he sure didn't see where her thinking of this was wrong.

"Want to explain that?" Jesse asked and then took a bite of one of the soft rolls and let the sweetness melt in his mouth. Butter, a little cinnamon, and a faint vanilla flavor. This was better than even a modern cinnamon roll. Wow.

"I have been thinking that Bushnell was finished with looking for new medals," Kelli said, shaking her head. "I thought he was done a few years ago. He isn't. He has never stopped, which would explain his trip here and his trip to Roosevelt. He's still tracking more of the medals."

"Lewis and Clark did make it all the way to the mouth of the Columbia River just north of here," Jesse said, understanding where she was going. "And they went through Idaho just north of the Roosevelt area."

Before she could say anything, there was a knock at the door.

They both looked at each other. More than likely just hotel staff, but the knock bothered Jesse.

He indicated that Kelli move around behind the door, then moved to the door and just barely opened it, making sure he was to one side ready to move if something came at him.

As he opened the door he got a real shock.

Standing there with his saddlebag over his shoulder was John Simon Bushnell.

Bushnell broke into a smile and said, "Thank god you two are here."

CHAPTER TWENTY-NINE

July 9th, 1906
Oregon Coast

WHEN KELLI HEARD the voice and the simple statement, she stepped out to see who had said that to Jesse. Seeing Bushnell standing there in his suit and vest and tie just flat stunned her.

What the hell was going on?

Bushnell nodded. "Doctor Rae, it is an honor to meet you for technically the first time. I am a fan of your books, including a couple you haven't written yet."

Kelli could feel her mouth open and then close.

Not a word even formed in her brain.

Jesse stood there, his hand on the door, just staring at Bushnell as well.

"May I come in?" Bushnell asked. "I can explain all this. Honest. Duster and Bonnie told me this would be a shock to you two at this point."

Jesse moved first and nodded that Bushnell should come in. Then Jesse looked both ways down the hallway before closing the door.

Bushnell turned to face Dr. Rae. "Your theory is correct. I am here to meet a ship's captain who might be willing to part with one of the Season Medals he picked up about twenty years ago. It will be the thirty-first I have recovered."

"Let's back up a long ways," Jesse said as Kelli just kept staring at the man.

Bushnell looked fairly old and weathered and his balding head had clearly seen far too much sun over the years. But on closer look at details, he clearly was a man of means.

Jesse indicated that Bushnell join them at the table overlooking the street and offered him a roll and some cookies, both of which Bushnell accepted with a "Thanks, haven't had breakfast yet."

Bushnell put his saddlebag down on the pine floor with a thump and then sat down.

So far Kelli hadn't been able to even form a sentence or a word, she was so shocked. From what she was gathering, the man she had been researching for this book was from the future as well.

How in the hell was that possible?

Then she remembered the picture where she had seen Jessie and Madison and Duster and herself and understood exactly the answer.

Jesse sat down, took a sip of his coffee and then looked at Bushnell as Kelli dropped back into her chair across from both of them.

"Start off with your real name in the future," Jesse said, "and when did you come through the crystal cavern?"

"I didn't come through the cavern," Bushnell said, his voice clearly happy. "You two and the original group are the last ones to use the cavern. I've never even seen the cavern or could find it if I tried. Have Duster and Bonnie tell you the story of how Carson Edwards was killed on the road leaving that cavern. Before you two joined. Damn scary stuff."

"So how the hell do you get back here?" Jesse asked.

Bushnell laughed. "For research, starting the year after you two joined up. We now all use the new institute out on Warm Springs Avenue in Boise. Bonnie and Duster and all of you built it together back in 1880 from my understanding. It looks like a big mansion, but has top state-of-the-art security and computers. The three levels of basements are amazing."

"How is that possible?" Kelli asked, finally getting her brain into gear.

Bushnell shrugged. "Time travel gives me a headache, but from what I understand, Bonnie and Duster and other mathematicians working for them figured out a way to take crystals and move them from the crystal cavern to the institute and then return them."

Jesse nodded, glancing at Kelli. "Did you notice the crystals on the ground by the door?"

"That cavern was just too overwhelming for me to remember much there," Kelli said.

"I sure would love to see it some day," Bushnell said. "But at this point, except for you fourteen originals, it's pretty much off limits and kept very secret."

"When did you come through?" Jesse asked. "And how many are now traveling in time for research?"

"Counting the three of us," Bushnell said, "there are thirty now. I first went through in 2019, but I am not allowed to tell you two anything that happens between 2016 and 2019, so don't ask. The institute has scary strict rules and you run it."

Bushnell pointed to Jesse and Kelli was shocked at how Jesse just sort of jerked backwards.

"Oops, probably wasn't supposed to tell you even that," Bushnell said. "Sorry."

Jesse nodded. "Yeah, let's be careful with that."

Bushnell nodded. "Got it."

"So you didn't tell us your real name," Kelli said.

"I am Doctor Kevin Bushnell from Michigan State University. We are allowed now to only use our real last names, but must change our first names on research trips."

Kelli was now really stunned. "Your first book on Early American Exploration was amazing."

"Well, thank you," Bushnell said, nodding and clearly embarrassed. "I obviously have learned a lot since that first book and am working on updating it given time."

He laughed at that joke.

"So you are back," Jesse said, "starting in 1880 gathering up Season Medals?"

"That was the idea," Bushnell said, nodding. "I figured the best way to get them into museums and back with the right Native American tribes was to gather them up, hide them until 2019, and then release them as a major find."

"My research showed that only three have surfaced," Kelli said.

"Yeah," Bushnell said, suddenly looking upset. The man clearly wore his emotions right out for anyone to see. "Three I could not get. But I'm afraid without your help, all the ones I have will not surface ever again."

"Why's that?" Jesse asked. "Hide them in a bad place?"

"I don't get the chance to hide them correctly," Bushnell said, now looking really down and depressed. "I've tried twenty times so far, and every time I have been killed before I get the chance to hide them correctly."

"Killed?" Jesse asked.

Kelli just sat forward, watching the man. He clearly was telling the truth and not at all happy about his story.

Bushnell nodded. "When you are killed in a past timeline, you end up back in the institute two minutes and fifteen seconds after you left. I keep coming back into the past, rounding up the medals, trying to outsmart whoever is killing

Some Classic Dean Wesley Smith Stories
Available at your favorite booksellers.

me and taking the medals. And for twenty different trips into the past, I have failed."

Again all Kelli could do was open her mouth and then shut it.

CHAPTER THIRTY

July 9th, 1906
Oregon Coast

JESSE SAT STARING at Bushnell. What the man was saying about being killed twenty times wasn't possible unless he was being followed by someone with intense resources and who was very, very good at what they did.

And Jesse doubted that was happening. More than likely this was just a crime of opportunity. And Bushnell just kept giving the guy an opportunity. But they were going to have to be careful just in case.

Jesse had to clear his mind of the time travel aspects of all this and just think inside this timeline. And think like an investigator.

"When do you buy the next medal," Jesse asked.

"Tomorrow," Bushnell said. "It's why I came here a day early to meet you two. Duster said you would be here and be able to help. Kind of embarrassing, telling him, to be honest. But after twenty failures, I had to ask permission to break the institute rules and talk with you."

Kelli looked at Jesse. "You don't think this is another time traveler doing this, do you?"

"No," Jesse said, and he didn't, but damned if he couldn't be sure it wasn't. At this point, he didn't know what to believe.

He just wished Duster and Bonnie had trained them a lot more about the past, not just how to survive, but about the ins and outs of time travel and timelines.

"Hadn't even thought of another researcher doing this sort of thing," Bushnell said. "In fact, I could walk down the street past numbers of them from my time period and not know them for who they are. And they wouldn't know me. Especially since I have aged twenty-six long years back here this trip."

"And you wouldn't know at all travelers who joined after you," Kelli said.

Jesse sat back, deciding right at that moment that things needed to change. He had only lived a year in the past and he could see massive problems coming in this setup.

"So what are you thinking?" Kelli asked Jesse, turning away from Bushnell.

"It only seems logical to me," Jesse said to Bushnell, "that our robber and killer is someone who follows you each time. And does it very well. Do you ever see him?"

"It's a guy wearing a dark overcoat and a black hood over his head with eyes cut through so he can see. The hood is tied with a string around his neck to hold it in place. And he wears miner's boots that are scuffed and ruff. I saw those boots a lot as I died each time."

Silence for a moment in the big suite.

"So what happens to the medals?" Kelli asked after a moment.

"More than likely melted down at some point along the way," Bushnell said, shrugging. "By someone who didn't know what they actually were."

"That would be a crime," Kelli said.

Bushnell nodded. "It's why I kept coming back. To try to stop that from happening."

Jesse didn't want to point out to Bushnell that if he hadn't collected all the medals, more than likely most of them would have survived just fine.

"So what do we do?" Bushnell asked.

"We do as we had planned on doing," Jesse said, looking at Kelli. "We recover the medals and make sure they get to our normal times."

"I would appreciate it if you stopped the killing part this time," Bushnell said. "Getting shot and killed is just not something a person can get used to even after twenty times."

"We'll try," Jesse said, smiling. He had every intention of stopping that part.

"So can we see the medals?" Kelli asked.

"They aren't here," Jesse said, clearly surprising her.

Kelli looked at Jesse with a frown.

Damn he was falling so in love with her, he couldn't believe it.

Bushnell nodded and pointed to his saddlebag. "That's a bag of quartz rocks I lug around that is close to the weight of the medals. The medals are in a bank safe deposit box in Portland. I get them on the way through headed for Roosevelt, Idaho, each time."

"And where exactly do the attacks happen?" Jesse asked. He knew the answer, but needed it confirmed.

"Always in the mountains around Roosevelt," Bushnell said. "I have one man I meet in Roosevelt in June of 1907 to get the last of the medals that I have been able to trace. He sells it to me and I never make it out of those mountains alive."

Jesse nodded. The miner's boots made sense. And now he was even more convinced that the crimes were just always a crime of convenience.

"So what do you normally do over the next year between now and then?" Kelli asked.

"For the last five trips back I've been working with another researcher. We are researching the riverboats and barges and such that took passengers on the Columbia to coastal towns like this one before the highways were built over the coastal mountain range. I spend the next year with him and then we will be done with that research."

Jesse nodded. He now had a plan and he knew where Bushnell's weak point was and how to stop the killer.

"We're going to leave tomorrow," Jesse said, "ahead of your meeting and meet you in Portland in a week at your bank."

Bushnell nodded.

Kelli nodded, watching him.

"We're going to switch out the medals there when you add the new one to your stash that you get from here," Jesse said. "We'll do it in the bank so in case someone is watching, no one will know."

"Okay," Bushnell said, but hesitantly.

"We are going to take the medals to Roosevelt and bury them under the floorboards of Janice and Steven's general store there in Roosevelt. About three feet down in the dirt."

Janice and Steven were two other researchers and part of the original fourteen, but this time they were there in the general store from another timeline. They had not come through with the bunch of them. But as Duster had told him when he introduced them, "No real difference at all."

"The flood will cover them," Bushnell said, looking worried.

Kelli laughed, finally understanding what Jesse was planning.

"The flood will protect them for a century or more," Jesse said.

"In 2019," Kelli said, "when you get back, you and I will be in charge of an expedition to dive and recover the medals as we put the final part of the mystery to bed."

Bushnell looked at her for a moment, then smiled. "I'll do the research nonfiction book about my distant relative who gathered up the medals and what it was like dealing with the Native Americans of the time, with a focus, of course on the Native Americans."

"And I'll do the historical crime book about the medals themselves," Kelli said, smiling. "And we'll reference each other's books and how we solved the mystery through our mutual research."

"Perfect," Bushnell said, his face beaming.

Jesse smiled at the smiling face of the woman he was falling head-over-heels for, and then at Bushnell.

"Only one problem," Jesse said. "We still don't really know who is doing this and killing you each time."

"Yeah, that would be nice to know," Bushnell said. "But if I have to take another bullet for the cause, I will. Don't want to, but I will."

"Now that's commitment to your research," Jesse said.

And the two researchers laughed.

Jesse wasn't so sure it was funny. In fact, he was completely convinced that something much deeper was going on. He just didn't know what.

But killing Bushnell so many times in so many places did not make sense in the slightest. And that had him worried more than he wanted to admit to the researchers.

PART FOUR
The Chase

CHAPTER THIRTY-ONE

June 2nd, 1907
Roosevelt, Idaho

KELLI WAS AMAZED that it had been almost a year now since Jesse came up with the plan while they were talking with Bushnell on the Oregon Coast. And so far, it seemed to be working fine.

She and Jesse had spent another night on the coast, mostly making love and enjoying the wonderful room.

Then, just before Bushnell finished buying the medal, she and Jesse had headed for Portland about four hours ahead of Bushnell.

She and Jesse had hidden up the trail in the coastal mountain range and had let Bushnell pass them, just to make sure no one was following him.

As Jesse had suspected, there wasn't. The robbery and murder and loss of the medals took place in Roosevelt.

But they had decided they were still going to take no chances.

They had made the transfer without a problem in the bank. Then she and Jesse had hauled the medals over to Roosevelt by train. She didn't even allow herself to look at them. She figured there would be more than enough time for that after they dug them up in 2019.

Jesse had figured how to fit the leather-wrapped medals into pockets inside his duster and in a money belt he had bought in Portland.

In Ontario, Oregon, they had left the train with the medals, purchased two horses, and headed for Roosevelt with the medals in a third saddlebag hidden underneath Jesse's main saddlebag.

They had made it all the way to Roosevelt by July 18th of last summer, transferred the medals into some oilskin bags, sealed them as best they could, and then buried them one late evening in Janice and Steven's general store under the floorboards and down into the dirt about two feet.

Jesse had asked Janice and Steven for permission, but not wanted them there for their own safety. And he had not told them anything about what they were doing.

They had agreed.

Then over the next few days, Jesse and Kelli had taken some rough measurements and markers so the underwater expedition in 2019 wouldn't have to dig up too much of the lake bottom.

With the medals safely stored for the future, both Jesse and Kelli had the rest of the summer and the entire winter to wait until Bushnell arrived in Roosevelt.

So they headed back to Boise, not to stay with Duster and Bonnie this time, but to stay in the wonderful mansion that Dawn and Madison had built right beside Bonnie and Duster's home.

Since Dawn and Madison were now living and running the Monumental Lodge on the summit above Roosevelt, their home they had built in Boise was free for the summer and winter.

The place was massive, with high ceilings in the entry and main room and dining room. Tall windows let in more than enough light and the tan and brown furnishings were picked by April, who had wonderful taste and knew how to make a room elegant, yet comfortable.

Dawn and Madison's master bedroom was huge and had a closet larger than Kelli's first dorm room in college. But both Kelli and Jesse didn't feel right staying in the master bedroom, so they took over the guest bedroom that had a featherbed that a person could get lost in without much problem.

To Kelli, the summer and winter and spring had been a magical time. She and Jesse just fit together, and both of them had enough projects that held their interest to keep them more than busy.

When the weather allowed, they went into the Idanha Hotel dining room for wonderful breakfasts. Kelli spent most of the days writing in notebooks in the library or at home, getting in as much detail about the history of the medals as she could, while Jesse spent afternoons in the downtown library and listening to old-timers in barber shops and bars tell stories of lost treasures and forgotten crimes.

He had gotten some great stories. A couple ideas Kelli was convinced would make great books after a ton of research.

During the evening, they had wonderful dinners together, usually both of them cooking and learning how to cook with what was available in the time.

Then there were the wonderful nights in a big featherbed.

The longer she spent with Jesse, the more convinced she was she wanted to spend even more time with him.

Years more, actually.

And in May of 1907, as they were packing to head up to Roosevelt, Jesse told her that he felt the same way.

They managed to get up to the Monumental Lodge by May 18th through large snow banks and then down into Roosevelt two days later and settled into the big house that Duster and Bonnie had built just up the stream from the main part of Roosevelt.

The big house was all logs, with a massive main room and three bedrooms in the back. The fireplace kept the house warm and comfortable.

On June 2nd, they finally really went to work as Bushnell arrived.

Jesse had given her lessons over the winter on tailing someone without being seen, and they planned on working together to see if they could spot the robber who would attempt to kill Bushnell.

Bushnell stayed in a cabin up a side creek about a half-mile above the town. He had told them he was always killed near that cabin, usually coming or going, usually within days of getting the last medal.

Kelli had asked Bushnell why he hadn't tried just staying up at the Monumental Summit Lodge and going down into Roosevelt for the meeting.

Bushnell had said that he had done exactly that. Twice. Both times he didn't make it back up the trail to the lodge.

Bushnell had seen them in Roosevelt right after he had arrived, nodded, but they had not talked to him as planned.

Now it was up to them to see if they could keep him alive.

CHAPTER THIRTY-TWO

June 19th, 1907
Roosevelt, Idaho

JESSE GLANCED OVER at Kelli, where she was sitting like a lady on a second story porch above a lawyer's office fanning herself in the hot afternoon. She had on her riding clothes and he knew her horse was saddled and waiting beside the building. Even from a distance like this, she was still beautiful. Over the last year he had come to love her more than he ever thought possible.

And he respected and admired her mind as well.

The narrow main street of Roosevelt, Idaho, was busy with a few roughly made carts and some men on horseback headed out leading pack horses covered in supplies. But from what Duster had said, this wasn't as bad as it used to be.

In the high days of this mining town, the main street would get so crowded, pack trains with supplies couldn't get through. And since no wagon could get in over the trails to this town, only rough carts made in the valley were seen.

But now, today, the sounds of the pianos playing in the saloons echoed from the open doors up through the valley. That music filled the valley every day and night in the summer. It had become a background sound for Jesse now.

Most of the men and the few women now in the valley were still working the mines or running other errands while the sun actually hit the valley floor.

With the steep and high mountains on both sides of the town, the sun wasn't a regular visitor to this valley. Even in the summer, the town got less than five hours of direct sunlight. The rest of the time the town was in a shadow as the sun lit the mountains around and above it.

Bushnell came out of the far saloon and headed toward the Monumental Stream that ran just past the town on the left. At this time of the year, the stream wasn't running fast enough to even pretend to do battle with the piano music.

Bushnell was dressed in his standard dark suit, vest, tie, and dark pants. He carried his saddlebag over his shoulder like he always did and it looked heavy.

A miner was waiting for him on a foot trail near the stream. The guy did not look dangerous at all to Jesse.

The miner and Bushnell talked for a moment. Then they both nodded and Bushnell handed the man a small bag, more than likely coins of some sort or small gold nuggets, and the man handed Bushnell something wrapped in cloth.

Bushnell opened it, nodded, shook the man's hand, tucked the prize in his saddlebag, and turned and headed for his horse.

The miner turned and went down the valley along the trail that was beside the creek, clearly having no more interest in Bushnell.

Now Bushnell had thirty-two of the Washington Peace Medals. Thirty-one were under the general store, the last one in his bag.

From what Jesse could tell, no one was following Bushnell at all.

Or even paying the slightest bit of attention besides him and Kelli.

Jesse mounted up and leisurely headed up the valley along the main road, watching for anyone that might be waiting for Bushnell.

He never saw anyone.

In this narrow valley, there just weren't a lot of places to hide since all the trees near the town itself had long ago been cut down.

So just before the side trail that led up to Bushnell's cabin, Jesse ducked into a stand of brush and tied up his horse. Then taking his rifle, he headed up through the brush and into the small side canyon, moving as silently as he could.

He finally reached a spot he had found ahead of time where he could see both the trail coming up and Bushnell's cabin. He got into position, making sure he was well-hidden.

Bushnell's cabin was a small log cabin tucked into some tall pine, clearly built by a miner to work a mine just up the stream. But that mine was now shut down and the tunnel caved in. The cabin had been abandoned and Bushnell had told Jesse he had bought it and the mining claim years ago to use.

He knew Bushnell would be coming up the trail and behind him Kelli would be watching to see who followed.

Jesse took a deep breath and scanned everything again. Now was the time they had been working for.

Why did he have a nagging doubt he was missing something and this just wasn't going to work.

Five minutes later, Bushnell came riding up the trail, his heavy saddlebags draped over his horse in front of him.

Jesse watched as Bushnell got off his horse just outside his cabin, looked around with a look of almost near panic on his face, and then headed into the cabin carrying his saddlebags.

Suddenly, a shot echoed through the narrow valley, clearly coming from the cabin.

"Damn! Damn! Damn!" Jesse said to himself as he scrambled at a fast run toward the cabin, his rifle in his hands and ready.

There was no back way into the cabin through the log walls, so he knew he had whoever was in there trapped.

The door still stood open and Bushnell was sprawled on the floor just inside the door.

A man stood over him, watching Jesse come running.

The man's hands were in the air and he was smiling.

Why in the hell would the man who had just killed Bushnell be smiling?

CHAPTER THIRTY-THREE

June 19th, 1907
Roosevelt, Idaho

KELLI HEARD THE shot while she was still a few hundred yards from the cabin. She kicked her horse into a fast run and grabbed her saddle rifle at the same time.

She came around the corner in the trail and saw Jesse moving slowly toward the open front door, his rifle drawn and pointing at someone inside the door.

Kelli skidded her horse to a stop and jumped off at a run, cocking a shell into the chamber of her lever-action. She went to Jesse's left to cover him as he moved closer to the door.

"He's not dead this time," a voice said from inside the cabin. "Since you're here finally. Got tired of killing the poor guy, actually, even though I know he doesn't die."

Kelli glanced at Jesse who just shook his head without really taking his eyes from the man inside the cabin.

"Come out into the daylight," Jesse said, his voice carrying a power that Kelli had not heard before. Jesse was not lowering his rifle in the slightest.

The man stepped out of the cabin, his hands up.

The strange man had no gun that Kelli could see. But Jesse didn't lower his gun, so she didn't either.

The strange man had short dark hair, wore a dark suit, dark vest, and black jeans and cowboy boots. Kelli noted that he had no hood or miner's boots or anything that Bushnell had described.

He saw Kelli and instead of being shocked, his eyes sort of lit up, clearly excited.

What the hell was going on here?

Why did he look familiar?

And why was he excited to see her?

The guy was clearly crazy.

Or he had help of some sort.

She did a quick scan of the narrow valley around them, studying the trees up the sides of the hill.

No one else she could see, but that didn't mean someone wasn't there.

"As I said," the man said. "I didn't kill poor old Bushnell this time. Just knocked him out so we could talk. He'll have a headache, but he'll be fine in a day. The gunshot was just to get your attention. I tossed the gun on the bed."

Kelli again scanned the area around the cabin for any help this nutcase might have.

"So what's your name?" Jesse asked.

"I can only tell you that my name is Bryant. I'm from the institute and the year 2110."

Kelli just shook her head.

Not two of them.

They had been stunned to learn that Bushnell was a traveler, but now the guy that had been killing him was as well.

And from a hundred years in the future.

She and Jesse hadn't told Bonnie and Duster about Bushnell being from the future because Bushnell had warned them not to.

So why were they now facing another traveler?

"I was starting to guess that something like this was happening," Jesse said, putting his rifle down.

"What?" Kelli asked, stunned at Jesse's response. Her rifle was still aimed at the Bryant guy.

"Even someone as inexperienced as Bushnell would have easily avoided the same guy from this timeline that many times," Jesse said. "But not if it was someone from the future stalking him for some reason."

"Oh," Kelli said, lowering her rifle.

Jesse glared at the smiling face of the man named Bryant. "What the hell is your reason?"

"I can only talk in very general terms," the man said. "I cannot contaminate the future by telling you about it. Major rule."

"Fine," Jesse said. "I understand that. Start where you can and tell us a story."

The man looked back at Bushnell sprawled inside the cabin, then indicated they move away from the cabin.

They all walked down the trail about twenty paces and then stopped. Kelli kept her gun down, but ready. Jesse didn't seem to be worried in the slightest, which she didn't understand at all. Over the last few years he had been the most careful person she had ever met, seeing things going on around them that she had completely missed. He was seeing something here as well that told him this guy was not a threat.

"In the early years of the crystal cavern and the institute," Bryant said, "only historical researchers and mathematicians were involved, thus the focus was either on the math or on the past, with no thought to the future at all."

"I'm involved now," Jesse said. "And I don't do either."

The man nodded. "Thankfully, yes."

Kelli wanted him to say more, but Bryant said nothing. Just kept smiling, glancing back and forth at both of them.

"Go on," Kelli said.

"I am authorized to tell you this much," Bryant said. "In 2019 your expedition to retrieve the Season Medals from Roosevelt Lake is successful and your book and Bushnell's book are successful."

"That seems to be a given," Jesse said. "If it is allowed to happen. Which I doubt it will be. Go on."

Kelli glanced at Jesse. He was clearly angry and she had never really seen Jesse angry while in the past before. The last time he was this angry was when he saw the picture and thought he was being duped by his good friends.

And she had no idea why he figured the medals being found wouldn't be successful.

"The medals are stolen in a robbery before they can be distributed," Bryant said. "Six innocent people are killed in that robbery."

"And that robbery happening changes just about every timeline going forward to 2110, doesn't it?" Jesse said.

Bryant nodded. "And not in a good way."

"How do you know all this?" Kelli asked.

"In one hundred years," Bryant said, "the math on all this has advanced to the point where it makes the fantastic breakthrough math that Bonnie and Duster are doing look like kids' algebra. And we have the computing power to trace the repercussions of any major event in history and most minor ones as well. In all major timelines."

"A robbery of some commemorative medals does not seem like a major event," Jesse said.

"I agree," Bryant said. "The medals were accidently destroyed in the process and we could not stop that, the robbery, or the deaths that occurred from our position in the future. At least not at the point of the robbery, or even slightly before."

"So your world sucks because of those six deaths," Jesse said. "And you are back here trying to stop the medals being even found."

Bryant nodded, now no longer smiling. "More billions die needlessly in billions of timelines because of those robbery deaths than I want to think about. In numbers of timelines, humans are basically wiped off this planet by events set in motion from those deaths during that robbery."

"All because we rescue some historical medals?" Kelli asked.

She wasn't really believing any of this, but of course, she was also standing in the Idaho mountains in 1907 and had lived for years back here while only two minutes passed in her real timeline. So belief at this point for her was a very relative term.

Jesse just shook his head.

"It's not really the medals as they stand," Bryant said. "It's the robbery of the medals after they are recovered from Roosevelt Lake. It is the deaths that cause the problem in the future timelines. All the deaths are collateral damage to the attempt to take the medals."

"So because Bushnell rounds up those medals instead of leaving them alone, the ripples forward through time are disastrous," Jesse said.

"Exactly," Bryant said.

"So you are trying to do a Monumental Summit Lodge switch of timelines," Jesse said.

Kelli glanced at him, feeling stunned. Bonnie and Duster had told them about what happened with the lodge, but that didn't mean she understood it. Clearly Jesse did.

"Yes," Bryant said simply.

"What do you want us to do?" Jesse asked.

"Get rid of the medals," Bryant said, "just as I did after each time I killed Bushnell."

"But you getting rid of the medals did not change the problem in your time, did it?"

"No," Bryant said. "Because Bushnell would just repeat his process again. So we need one more thing done. When Bushnell returns to the institute after this attempt and the medals can't be found in the lake, ban him from collecting them again."

"I can ban him?" Jesse asked.

Kelli was surprised at that as well, but said nothing.

"Just trust me and do it," Bryant said.

"If this works this way, how will you know?" Kelli asked.

"I will know instantly when I return to my time," Bryant said. "Did Bonnie and Duster explain the shimmering to you after they returned from building the Monumental Summit Lodge?"

"They described it like a heat wave without heat that only lasted a second," Kelli said.

"That's a time wave as time streams simply reset and adjust into the future. Time and matter and space are fluid and connected."

"And you will be able to remember the other time streams?" Kelli asked.

"I will, and a few others who are in the institute in my time as well."

A moaning came from the cabin and Bryant turned and looked worried. "I need to get out of here. Just tell him you chased me off. And please tell no one you met me. Not even Bonnie and Duster. This must remain our secret until you both die."

"Pretty strong request," Jesse said.

Bryant nodded. "I hope you do what we are asking. In all the years of the institute, this is only the third time we have adjusted time streams like this. Doing so is so against all that we believe and that the institute stands for. But this was critical and this is our only chance with this adjustment."

Bryant glanced back at the cabin and then faced them again.

"It really isn't though, is it?" Jesse asked, laughing. "You are not a good liar."

Bryant also laughed and the laugh sounded almost the same as Jesse's laugh to Kelli as the sounds echoed up through the canyon.

And now she understood why this guy looked familiar.

"No, it isn't," Bryant said. "This was just the easiest, even killing poor Bushnell in there a bunch of times to get your attention. Problem was that he didn't tell anyone what was happening until this last time, so Bonnie and Duster couldn't help him or stop him."

"Seems like the institute needs a reporting system or two," Jesse said, shaking his head.

Bryant laughed again. "Researchers, can't live with them, can't live without them."

Sounds came from the cabin as Bushnell struggled to stand up.

"It was wonderful meeting you both. A dream come true for me," Bryant said.

With that, he tapped something beside his ear and vanished without a sound.

Jesse and Kelli just stood there, staring at each other.

Finally Jesse sighed. "We tell no one. About him or Bushnell in there."

Kelli nodded as they turned toward the cabin to help Bushnell.

"I agree," Kelli said. "And besides, who would believe us if we told them we just met our great-great-grandson."

That stopped Jesse cold in his tracks and she just kept walking and laughing.

CHAPTER THIRTY-FOUR

December 3rd, 1907
Roosevelt, Idaho

JESSE USED THE break in the weather to bundle up in two layers of coats and two pairs of pants to take a ride up the valley to Bushnell's cabin. The sun was shining, but it added no heat at all to the biting cold air. Jesse could see every breath he or his horse took.

The towering white-covered mountains that stretched above him on both sides felt comforting.

There was no one moving at all in the valley. The silence seemed almost like a weight. Isolation didn't begin to describe this area of the country.

Bushnell was long gone. He had left in the summer right after he had been hit on the head, taking the one medal with him.

Jesse knew that he would see Bushnell the moment after he arrived back in the institute in Boise in two years. Of course, the institute wasn't built yet and Jesse knew he had many lives to live before those two years of real time passed.

127

And there was a lot of work to do in real time, from what he was gathering.

He and Kelli had told Janice and Steven they would run their general store for them through the winter. Since the Roosevelt area only had about a hundred people in the valley during the winter, there wasn't much to do, and Janice and Steven were happy to let them stay since they had survived seven winters in this valley already. They were ready for a break.

Bushnell's small log cabin in the snow looked very sad, almost buried up to its eaves, not even protected by the tall pine trees around it.

Jesse tied his horse up to a small pine sticking out of the snow near the cabin front and waded through the knee-deep snow to the heavy log door and pushed it open.

There had been no tracks in the snow from anyone else since it started snowing.

There was very little inside the small cabin. Just a mattress against one wall stripped of all blankets, a cold stone fireplace that felt even colder without a fire going in its black mouth.

The windows were holding against the weight of the snow and the winter winds, but didn't let in much light because they were covered from the outside. A clean sink sat to the left side of the cabin under one window and a few chairs were around a rough wooden table.

Most of the light came from the open door, but that was enough for now.

He thought about building the fire, but decided it wasn't worth the effort. He was warm enough in his coats for the moment.

And more than likely this was just a wild goose chase after all. He had told Kelli he was looking for a safe place to make sure the medals were lost for good.

But Jesse had a hunch he would find something better to do with them, and that came from a comment Bushnell himself had made.

"Kelli know you are here?" a voice said behind him.

Jesse turned around to face Duster.

Only not the Duster he knew, but a Duster aged to almost sixty.

Duster still wore the same coat and hat and it clearly looked like Duster, just an older version.

So the message had been accurate. Right to the time of day. Just not sent by the person who Jesse thought had sent it.

"She does," Jesse said. "But she thinks I'm just out to check on the cabin here, find a place to bury the medals, and get some air. She did not see the message."

"This valley can be claustrophobic at times," Duster said, nodding. "Glad you understood the message."

"But from my understanding," Jesse said. "You can't be here, since you are also in Boise right now. You know, the old two of the same people in the same spot kind of time travel problem."

Duster smiled and laughed. "First trip back into the past and you already understand it better than most."

Duster reached over and put his hand through the countertop.

"Let me guess," Jesse said. "Hologram from your time sent back here."

Duster again nodded.

"I thought that was Bryant that left the message," Jesse said.

In the sink in a red blood-like ink a date and time had been written. Written under the date, "Jesse, meet me, please."

"That kid is way after my time is gone," Duster said. "But you told me about what happened here about ten years ago my time, even though you promised not to. I sent an assistant to come in quickly, write the message and get out while you were talking to the kid out front."

"Okay," Jesse said. "But why?"

"Because when you told me about meeting the Bryant kid from the future and what he had done, you and I talked about doing this in my time."

"Not too much information," Jesse said, holding up his hand. "I already know too much."

Duster nodded. "Something came up that I needed to talk with you now, before you go back and get going with everything we do together going into the future. I figured this was as good a place as any."

"Might as well get me while I am still confused," Jesse said, laughing.

Duster laughed at that as well. "I've known you for a very long time now and I can't remember ever seeing you confused."

"I cover it well," Jesse said.

Duster shook his head. "The future is a grand place. And this conversation won't be that long and you can't tell me about this meeting until June 8th of 2058. It's June 7th for me."

"Okay," Jesse said, shaking his head. "I think I'll just forget about it until you mention it to me."

Duster shook his head sadly. "You can't forget this. That's the reason I'm here."

Jesse just stared at the hologram of the older version of his boss for a moment. "Either something horrible happens, such as with the medals, or you are here for something else."

"I'm here," Duster said, "because this can never happen. What has happened to you during this trip into the past can never happen going into the future to any other timeline travelers."

"You mean meeting three other time travelers from the future counting you?"

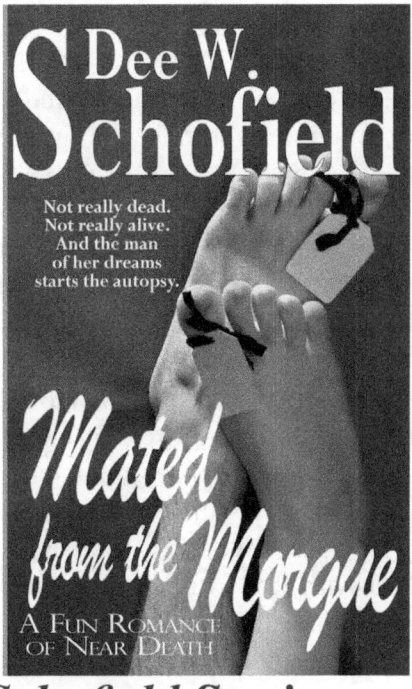

Some Classic Dee W. Schofield Stories
A Pen Name of Dean Wesley Smith
Available at your favorite booksellers.

"Exactly," Duster said, nodding. "I'm not going to tell you what happens as we go forward together, but make sure this sort of thing has a firm rule against it. Convince me and Bonnie without telling me about this conversation."

"Oh, that's going to be easy," Jesse said, shaking his head.

"Maybe not, but it is critical," Duster said. "What has happened to you on this trip cannot happen to anyone going forward. The world is a very lucky place because this happened to you and not someone else."

"And since you can't tell yourself to fix it, you have to tell me," Jesse said. "But I'm betting that hologram could go back and tell yourself a ton of stuff."

Duster laughed. "There is a real reason I tell you this that you will discover over time."

Jesse waved that off. "I assume there is a mathematical reason for this as well, since this is coming from you in the distant future," Jesse said.

Duster nodded "We just developed the next level of timeline math. And have the computers to crunch the immense amount of data."

Duster shook his head.

"Tired of playing god?" Jesse asked.

Duster jerked and then nodded. "It is not our place to direct the future of trillions of lives. We only research the past as it existed and leave the future the hell alone."

"That seems to be more than enough," Jesse said. "I can almost understand the mess Bushnell did with coming back and simply trying to save those medals."

"And with that I agree," Duster said. "So make sure the rule sticks. Now I'm going to get out of here before I slip and say something that will cause more problems."

With that he vanished like turning off a light without so much as "I'll see you in forty plus years."

The cabin was empty and cold and silent once again.

Clearly the technology had gotten a lot better than plugging in wires to a wooden box in a cave. And the hologram technology was clearly off the charts better.

Jesse went about making sure that nothing had been disturbed in the cabin, then he pulled the door closed and climbed back on his horse in the bright sunshine that reflected off the pure white snow.

The bitingly cold winter day was beautiful, with the air crisp and clear, the snow sparkling, and the mountains like walls to his own private world.

If he wasn't actually living in 1907, after all this he'd be laughing all the way to the nearest bar.

CHAPTER THIRTY-FIVE

April 22nd, 1908
Roosevelt, Idaho

KELLI WATCHED AS Jesse dug in the frozen dirt under Janice and Steven's store.

They had carefully removed the floorboards and now Kelli was using an old blanket to contain the dirt that Jesse was managing to break out of the ground with a pick and shovel. They were going to have to put all this back so for a year no one could tell they had done anything to the floor.

They had closed the store early and outside it was snowing hard, so no one was going to venture out or disturb them in any way. There were still less than a hundred people in the entire valley, and Jesse and Kelli knew the patterns of them all.

At first, when the first snows closed the valley, Kelli thought she was going to hate being trapped in such a deep, dark, cold place for eight months. But their cabin was comfortable, the people friendly, and she and Jesse had come to love each other even more.

Amazing how being that close day and night could really strengthen a relationship. Either that or kill it. But they had been lucky and the time alone together had made their relationship stronger by a long ways. They had enjoyed every minute of being together. And she had no doubt they were going to be together off into the future.

And a lot more trips into the past as well.

Jesse seemed to pace himself just fine as he dug, resting often and declining Kelli's offer to help. They had decided that they needed to get the Season Medals out of the ground before there was any chance of anyone coming in over the pass.

They planned on leaving the bag in the ground to be found in 2019 by the dive expedition. Only with no medals in it, just some metal pans to help with metal detectors doing the searching.

They had not decided what to do with the Season Medals yet. But both of them wanted time to look at them before deciding.

One solution that Jesse had suggested was that they bury them next spring in the path of the landslide that came in across the valley and created Roosevelt Lake. That way the medals would be under a hundred feet of rock and mud and by 2019 a huge forest grew on the mudslide.

That was a decent idea, but she hated doing that.

And Jesse had said he did as well. But at the moment it was the best solution they had talked about.

After almost an hour, Jesse finally got to the bag and worked it loose from the frozen ground, putting it on the blanket next to the dirt he had shoveled out.

Then he stood and took a drink of water from a cup on the counter and nodded to Kelli.

"Unwrap them."

"You think they are actually in this bag?" Kelli asked,

Jesse laughed. "After what has happened this trip so far, I'm making no bets."

He hadn't told her about his visit from the holographic Duster. He figured that was just better left between him and Duster years from now.

She took the frozen saddlebag to the big sink in the back room of the store and slowly poured hot water that she had been heating on the stove in pots over the bag.

It took three pots of hot water before she could finally open the bag and another full pot before she could pull out the first clump of medals.

She dropped them into another pot of lukewarm water to both clean and thaw them slowly.

After about five minutes, she held up one to show it to Jesse.

It was a medal quite a bit larger than a silver dollar and had very little wear on it. It shone bright, sparkling silver in the lamplight because it was wet.

On one side of the medal were stamped words surrounded by an olive branch on the left and maple leaves on the right. The reverse side of the medal showed a farmer sowing crops in a field.

"We can't destroy these," Kelli said. "These are the Season Medals. Only just over three hundred were originally made and almost none survive."

"And we can't let the world know they exist, either," Jesse said. "If Bryant is correct. At least not for some years of real time."

Kelli nodded. The wonderful medals in her hands were major parts of history. As a researcher of history, her job was not to destroy history, but to find the truth and document it.

She would be willing to end her book on a simple statement after the lake dive expedition came up empty.

"With luck, the great lost treasure of the Season Medals will someday be found."

But she couldn't make herself guarantee they would never be found. Ever.

Jesse put his arms around her, looking at the medals. "Remember that Bushnell said no one but us *originals* even knew where the mine and crystal cavern are located."

"You thinking we take them back to the cavern and leave them in there?" Kelli asked, turning in Jesse's arms and looking into his eyes. The idea excited her more than she wanted to admit. At least there they would be safe for a very long time.

"I do," he said, smiling at her. "We just got to get them out of this valley and to the cavern without telling anyone what we are doing."

She kissed him, loving the idea and loving him. Then she looked up at him again. "Do we tell anyone when we get back to the cavern?"

"No," Jesse said. "At least not for a decade or more. But I'm betting Duster will guess because we'll need his help a little. While you keep everyone else entertained, I'm going to take the medals and stash them. I know a perfect spot."

She nodded again and kissed him again. Then she pushed him back slightly before they got too hot. "Thank you for honoring the past."

"It seems," Jesse said, "since we are going to be living and working in the past a great deal, it's the least I can do."

CHAPTER THIRTY-SIX

June 8th, 1908
Roosevelt, Idaho

JESSE STOOD NEXT to Duster and Madison and Kelli on one of the board sidewalks of Roosevelt that ran from the general store on down to some saloons that were banging out piano music that sounded desperate.

The town was dying. Of that there was no doubt. Most of the mines had played out or never found color at all, and one of the big mills hadn't bothered to even bring in the big boilers to start up the place, even though it was built and lumber was cut for the fires.

A number of stores were boarded up and the town's only lawyer had not come back for the summer.

In a few years, if the town had been left alone, it would have been a ghost town, Jesse had no doubt. But the town didn't even have that long to live.

A huge mudslide would come down the nearby Mule Creek and fill the entire valley to the depth of over a hundred feet, backing up the spring runoff behind it and forming a lake over Roosevelt.

The lake would be named Lake Roosevelt.

Jesse and Duster and everyone else had no desire to stay another winter and watch the destruction. It was about time to leave, head back to Boise, and then after a few months, back to the mine and then the future.

Their real present.

Kelli and Jesse had their winter home here locked up and the extra supplies were on two packhorses. Next spring the home would go under water as well.

Duster and Madison had come down from the lodge to help them get up the trail.

Kelli and Jesse had the medals in money belts strapped under their clothes and in secret pockets in their saddlebags. There was no way to tell that they were carrying thirty-one rare medals between them. To Jesse, he liked the feel of them against him.

It felt as if he was doing something special, something important.

And from what he gathered about his job going forward, and he and Duster creating the Institute, his work would continue to be important.

The four of them had just come out of Janice and Steven's general store after saying goodbye. The sun was warm, the day about as good as it got in this remote and deep valley.

They had all stopped, standing in the sun, sort of taking in the almost dead town one last time. Kelli leaned around behind Madison and said, "Cameraman on the wagon."

Jesse laughed as he looked up.

It was clear the photographer had just taken the photo that would start all this between him and Kelli.

The photographer wore a dark suit with a narrow-brimmed hat. He had his camera set up on a four-legged tripod in the back of a rough supply wagon to get it up off the ground. He had the wheels of the wagon locked into place and the wagon bed braced with logs to keep it from even slightly moving.

The reason Kelli had her back slightly to the camera in the photo was because she had leaned back to tell Jesse about the camera.

"Let's get going," Duster said, laughing, "before he gets more pictures that will get us all in more trouble."

Kelli moved over and kissed Jesse.

"Wouldn't it have been something if I had found a picture of us doing that?" she asked.

"I think it worked out just fine the way it was," Jesse said.

"I completely agree," she said. "And when we get back, I'm framing that picture and hanging it on a wall in our home."

"We're going to have a home?" he asked. "I've only known you for a day."

"Damn right we are, mister," she said, laughing. "And as I keep telling you, I've had quicker."

With that, they all mounted up and turned their back on Roosevelt, Idaho, headed up the valley toward the Monumental Summit Lodge.

Jesse had no doubt he would be back here at some point. He had no idea what this past, or any past in his future held.

He glanced over his shoulder and for a moment he thought he could see Lake Roosevelt, beautiful and clear and bright blue, covering the town like a mirage in the sun.

Then the image shifted and the dying mining town returned.

At least for a short time.

CHAPTER THIRTY-SEVEN

July 15th, 2016
Above the ghost town of Silver City, Idaho

KELLI AND JESSE and Bonnie and Dawn were all sitting in Bonnie's big kitchen in Boise waiting. Madison and Duster had left yesterday for Silver City to pull the plug on this trip into the past.

April and Ryan were in their home waiting in their kitchen.

For the past hour, she and Jesse had their saddlebags on their laps with her notebooks, his research stuff on past crimes, and the hidden Season Medals.

Not a person had asked what they had done with them.

And they had told no one about Bushnell being a traveler or that they had met a traveler from a far distant future.

Bonnie and Duster knew the plan for the medals being under Janice and Steven's general store. That was fine for now.

No one else needed to know the rest of the details.

One thing for certain, there was nothing about the Season Medals that had been boring.

And because of them, she had met the love of her life.

Bonnie and Duster's big mansion around them was dark and closed up. Horses were all sold off and a caretaker had been hired to watch the house and clean a few times a week.

Dawn and Madison were planning on coming back to this point in time in this timeline in a month, so their house was closed up, but not as tightly as this house. Kelli wasn't sure how that would work, but Bonnie assured her it would.

Dawn and Madison wanted to spend more of a lifetime in the lodge. Then they would return and join the others for lunch in the mine.

Kelli was once again having trouble understanding that she and Jesse had spent all this time, these years, in the past and only just over two minutes had really elapsed. And Dawn and Madison could come back and spend another forty or fifty years and for them only another two minutes would pass.

The idea of it all just made her mind go numb.

She wasn't sure if she would ever get used to the idea. But she certainly planned on taking advantage of it many, many times.

Bonnie glanced at her gold pocket watch and tucked it back in her pocket. "It's nine a.m. They should be in the mine by now. Everyone get ready."

Kelli put her saddlebag over her shoulder at the same time as Jesse did.

Bonnie and Dawn also put saddlebags over their shoulders, holding onto them with one hand.

A moment later they were all standing with one hand on the wooden box in the crystal cavern.

Eight of them were crowded around the wooden box on the table. Bonnie and Duster and Ryan and April and Madison had left years earlier, but they had all come back together.

"Well, that was an interesting two minutes," Duster said, stepping back out of the crowd as Madison put on a glove and only unhooked one wire from the machine, leaving the wires connected to the same crystal.

"I got the men's shower first," Duster said. He turned with a saddlebag over his shoulder and headed for the open door to the supply cavern.

Kelli had stepped back and just stared at the huge place. The beauty of the billions of crystals was almost too much for her mind to grasp.

"You all mind if I take the women's shower?" Madison said after kissing Dawn. "Long dusty ride."

"Be our guest," Bonnie said.

Kelli just kept staring at the intense beauty of the crystal cavern towering over them.

Jesse was standing beside her and he reached over and took her hand.

"It's real," he said.

She nodded, just staring around at the billions of crystals and how the cavern seemed to disappear off into the distance.

"And only just over two minutes passed in all that time we spent back there," Kelli said.

Jesse laughed. "I don't think we spent it. As far as I'm concerned, we enjoyed it."

She looked up into his handsome smiling face and squeezed his hand. "I agree and stand corrected."

With that, they turned for the supply cavern following Dawn and Bonnie and April and Ryan.

At the door, Jesse pointed to the few hundred crystals stacked and glowing beside the door where the door had been cut into the cavern.

Kelli nodded. "It seems we have work to do right here in this timeline, don't we?"

"That we do," Jesse said.

They went to one of the big tables and worked at changing clothes into the modern clothes it seemed like they hadn't worn in a very long time. To Kelli, the jeans and blouse felt normal, but the tennis shoes just felt strange after years of women's shoes in the past and cowboy boots.

They were the last ones in the cavern when they moved all the medals to one saddlebag.

Kelli nodded to him and he smiled.

She was so thankful they were doing this.

"I want you with me when I hide these," Jesse said.

Kelli glanced up at him. "What are you worried about?"

"Because if anything ever happened to me, these medals are far, far too valuable to be lost again."

She kissed him and he put the bag on the ground under one table.

Then the two of them headed for the kitchen area, arm-in-arm.

CHAPTER THIRTY-EIGHT

July 15th, 2016
Above the ghost town of Silver City, Idaho

JESSE LET DAWN use the men's showers and April went for the women's showers while Bonnie started on something for them to eat with Ryan helping.

After Duster looked like he was settled, Jesse motioned for him. "We need to ask you a question or two if we could."

Jesse, holding Kelli's hand, turned and headed back into the supply cavern.

Duster followed and when Jesse got back to the table, he turned to face Duster. "We got one thing to deal with, and something major to talk about."

Duster nodded, clearly looking worried as he glanced between the two.

"I need you to make sure I am not setting off any of your hidden alarms down the tunnel, but we would rather, at this point, you not come with us."

"Going outside?" Duster asked, frowning.

"No," Jesse said. He picked up the heavy saddlebag with the Season Medals in it. "We just need to hide something for a decade or two real time, and since so few of us know about this place, I figured this would be the best and safest place in the world."

Duster smiled, nodded, and moved over to where there was a hidden panel on the wall and flicked off three switches, showing Kelli and Jesse what they were.

"No cameras on?" Jesse asked.

"None," Duster said, showing him the controls for those as well.

Jesse picked up a shovel from a stack of them and then holding Kelli's hand, they headed down the tunnel, the heavy saddlebag over his shoulder.

"We'll only be a minute," Kelli said.

Duster nodded and turned his back.

They went down the tunnel and then turned into the side tunnel. From the looks of it, Duster had reinforced the dead-end fake tunnel for a good thirty paces to make it look like everything else.

Jesse checked the end of the tunnel to make sure it wasn't a hologram, then he turned and walked ten paces back up the tunnel to about where Kelli stood looking nervous.

"Have I said how much I hate mine tunnels?" she asked.

He laughed and kissed her. "Almost done."

He finally found an opening above one of the large timbers and under the dirt above it. He tucked the saddlebag up there on top of the huge beam, making

sure it couldn't be seen from either direction, pushing it back with the handle of the shovel.

He pointed back at the corner and Kelli followed his direction.

Then he silently counted the beams back to the one where the bag was hidden.

"Fourteen beams," he said. "Same number as the originals who know about this place."

"I can remember that," she said, smiling.

They headed back up the tunnel and through the two hologram walls to where Duster waited. He still had his back to the tunnel when Jesse put the shovel back in the pile and then picked up a heavy pair of gloves from another table.

"That can't be found for at least a decade or more," Jesse said.

"I'm assuming there is something I missed," Duster said, "about your adventure with Bushnell and the Season Medals."

"Given time," Jesse said, "We'll tell you all about it. But first, we have something else to talk about."

Duster nodded. "You had a hell of a first trip I gather."

"More than you can know at this point," Jesse said.

Even Kelli looked at him funny when he said that.

Jesse motioned for Duster to come with him and they walked together back down the short tunnel and into the impressive crystal cavern. He didn't let the incredible beauty distract him this time.

Jesse took two steps inside and turned and pointed to the pile of crystals on the ground.

He put on the thick pair of gloves and gently picked up one crystal from the pile.

It was surprisingly heavy and glowed in his hands.

He held it away from his body for a moment as Duster watched, then gently returned it to the pile.

"I watched your fear of someone finding this place when we came in," Jesse said. "And after experiencing all this and the past, I totally and completely agree."

"There are fourteen of us who know about this place," Jesse said. "That needs to be the limit for here."

Duster frowned, but said nothing.

Jesse went on. "We need to build a top secret place in Boise and take those crystals and others from the wall and that machine and move this operation to Boise."

Duster looked at him with this strange look.

"You'll have to figure out if the crystals will work from there, but I'm betting they will," Jesse said. "Besides those of us who already know about this cavern, no one new should ever be allowed to come here again."

Duster nodded, so Jesse just kept pushing.

"We build a mansion out on Warm Springs with three layers of secret underground research and computer and crystal areas," Jesse said.

Duster again nodded.

"And instead of just tossing history majors into the past with no training, we train them before they go and give them strict rules, such as no one can talk to anyone from the future in the past. For example, Kelli and I can't go back into the past on our own and track you down and talk to you before this."

Duster looked at Jesse and Kelli. "You two had a hell of a few years back there I see."

"I'm not a mathematician or a history major," Jesse said. "You hired me to make sure people were vetted and the type of people you want. You hired me to see things. That's what I do."

DEAN WESLEY SMITH

USA Today **Bestselling Author**

the **First Tee Panic**

AND OTHER VERY REAL GOLF STORIES

Former PGA Golf Professional and USA Today *bestselling writer Dean Wesley Smith walks you step-by-step, club-by-club from your car to the first tee and beyond in a laugh-out-loud style that not only teaches, but entertains.*

A perfect gift for the golfer in your family.

Now Available **from all your favorite booksellers in trade paper and electronic editions.**

Duster nodded.

"So now that I know about all this and have spent some years back in the past, I can see just a few of the problems going forward. Hire me to pay attention to the future and give the rest of you the freedom to pay attention to the mathematics and the past."

Duster smiled and reached out his hand. "Damn, Bonnie and I were hoping for just that. And this idea for a place in Boise solves all sorts of problems."

Jesse shook Duster's hand.

"I suppose you even have a name made up for it," Duster said, smiling?"

Jesse just laughed. "How about The Historical Research Institute? Just the Institute for short."

"Damn," Duster said, nodding. "I like it."

"This is wonderful," Kelli said, hugging Jesse's arm.

Duster looked at Jesse "I think you just got yourself a hell of a job."

"It will certainly be interesting," Jesse said, smiling.

They turned and headed back into the supply cavern with Duster leading.

"Now, if the crystals work outside of this cavern," Jesse said, "I have some ideas of what we can do to build a very, very safe and hidden place. But we're going to need all fourteen of us originals involved to build it in 1880 in a lot of different timelines."

Duster just laughed. "I love the excitement. But how about we have some lunch first?"

Kelli hugged Jesse and they both laughed as they walked toward the kitchen area.

"I guess there's always time for lunch," Jesse said.

With that, Kelli stopped him and kissed him hard while trying not to laugh.

She pretty much succeeded.

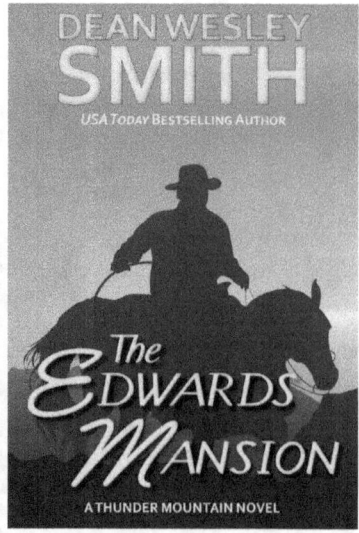

The First Three Thunder Mountain Novels
Available at your favorite booksellers.

Coming Next Issue in Smith's Monthly
A return to the Thunder Mountain Series in a brand new novel.

WARM SPRINGS

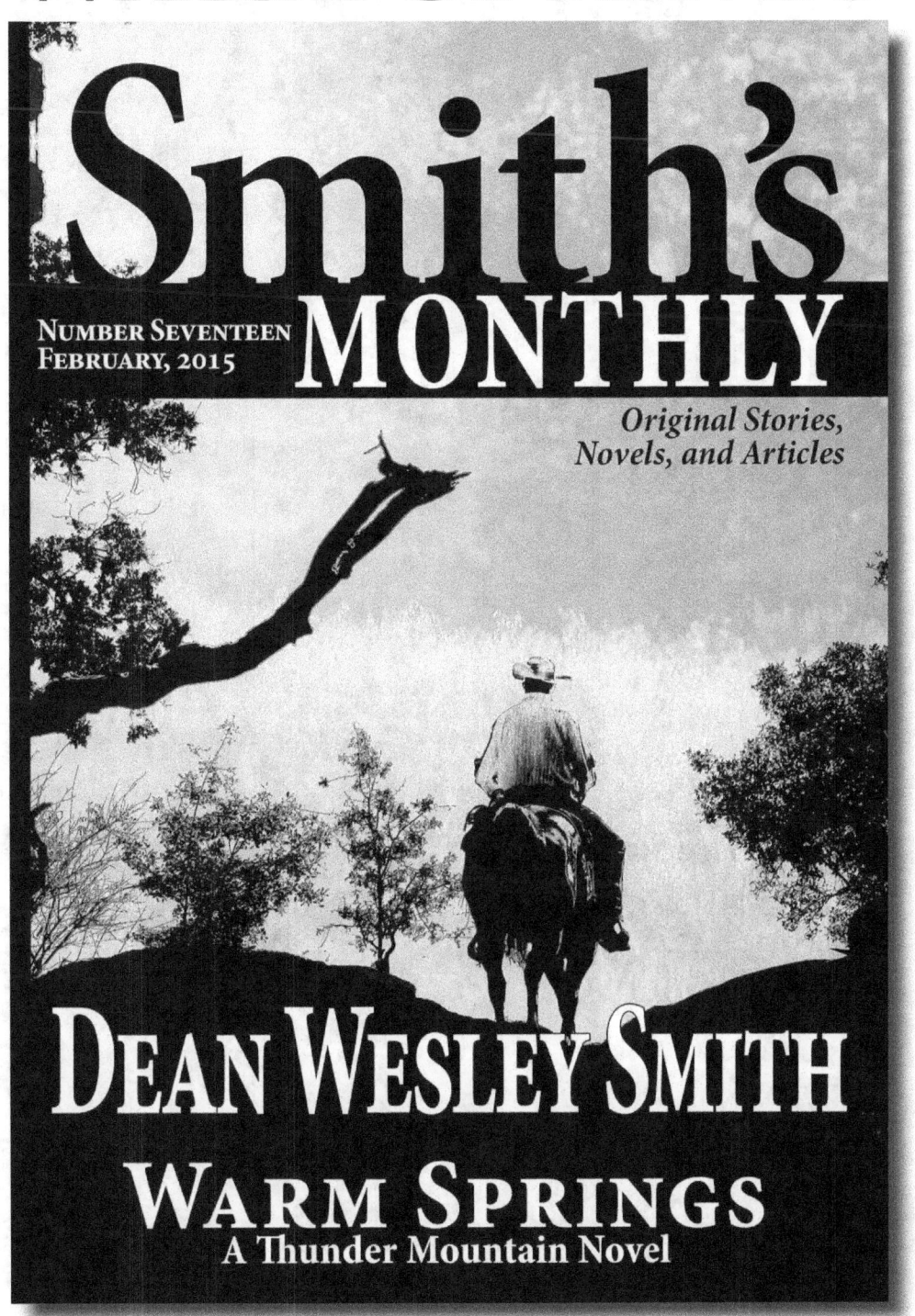

#1... October 2013

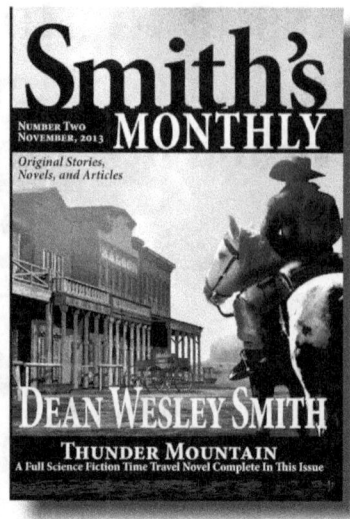

#2... November 2013

#3... December 2013

#4... January 2014

#5... February 2014

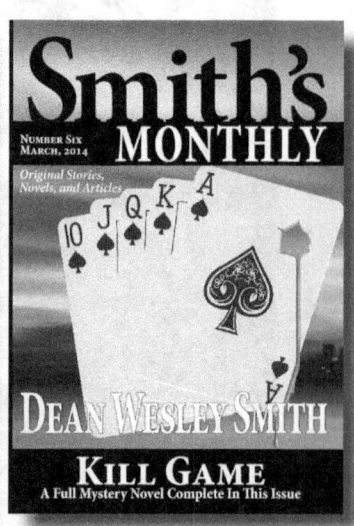

#6... March 2014

#7... April 2014

#8... May 2014

#9... June 2014

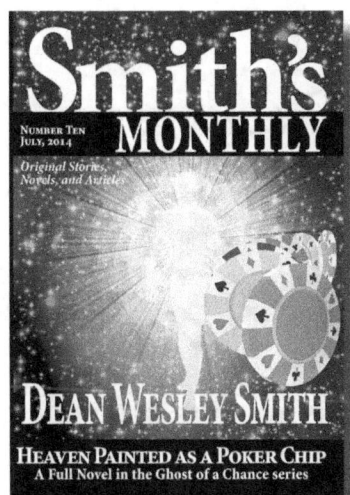

#10... July 2014

#11... August 2014

#12...September 2014

#13...October 2014

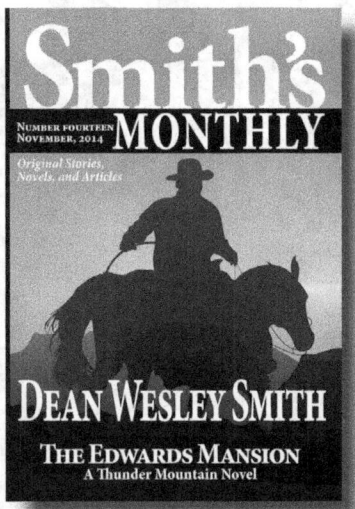

#14...November 2014

#15...December 2014

The First Fifteen Issues of Smith's Monthly!!!

Subscribe Now and start with any issue.
All issue are available from all your favorite booksellers in trade paper and electronic editions.

www.smithsmonthly.com

Subscribe:	*Electronic* Subscription:	*Paper* Subscription:
	6 Issues... $29.99	6 Issues... $59.99
	12 Issues... $49.99	12 Issues... $99.99

Available Now!
From all your favorite booksellers in trade paper and electronic editions.

USA TODAY BESTSELLING AUTHOR

DEAN WESLEY SMITH

HEAVEN PAINTED
as a Christmas Gift

A GHOST OF A CHANCE NOVEL

www.ingramcontent.com/pod-product-compliance
Lightning Source LLC
Chambersburg PA
CBHW081153170626
46813CB00009B/3175